THE MUSIC DISC MURDER

ITI Music Corporation Publishing
16057 Tampa Palms Blvd West, Tampa, FL 33647

Other Novels: "Circle of Chance"

Registered with Library of Congress 2018

ISBN: 978-0-9995684-2-2

Creative Editor: Laura Evaneski

Cover: RoxC LLC/www.roxc.graphics/Roxanne Clapp

Author Photo: Patricia Johnson

Cover Photo: Canva.com

To My Wife, Laura, the journey continues. You have kept me inspired as I continue to weave stories. Thank You. Much, Much, Love to you as we continue down this path.

To My Daughter, you continue to amaze me. I love you, dearly!

Thanks to family and friends as I share my past and future with you all. Most times, the story writes itself, and I am just the vehicle putting it to paper.

Please enjoy.

The Music Disc Murder
Chapter 1

Richard sat on his gold-tone leather couch at 9:10
PM, with a Winston cigarette being drawn from his
lips as he exhaled. The Pabst Blue Ribbon beer, in his
other hand, was dripping with water as he pulled it
from the ice chest on the grey carpet. He stared at
the two guys, almost through them, sitting across
from him, and then gulped down his third can.

Angrily, out loud, he asked the question, "Well, is
anyone else going to come to my celebration and
birthday party?"

Unfortunately, sitting in the two chairs facing Richard,
were his two closest friends from work, Stewart and
Paul, who were high from smoking a joint. They
looked back at him and shrugged their shoulders in
dismay. Richard groaned and guzzled down more
beer, his mind fending off his disgust.

Looking at each other, the two guys got up off their
chairs and strolled into the kitchen, where they found
the red-velvet cake and pretzels. Needless to say,
they ate most of it, in their present state.

By 10 PM, all hope was gone whether anyone else
was going to attend the party, and the two guys said
goodnight and headed home. Then, as usual, Richard
continued his outburst of pity and rage to an empty
apartment as he drank himself into another restless
night of sleep.

It was just like Richard to send out invites on the prior Wednesday to all regarding his promotion party celebration. And he did so painstakingly to make sure that his party was a success. He even posted flyers at the office on Friday as a reminder, so everyone didn't forget about his promotion to the Corporate Office. He also invited a few of the new people that he would be working with, even if he only met them when he was hired and didn't have a chance to build a relationship at this point.

Smiles from most of the employees and the profound nodding of "yes" to his question, "Are you coming to my party," came from the mouths of all those he asked. However, this was Saturday night, and as usual, it turned out to be a disaster.

"Why he kept asking himself, Why?"

By all rights, Richard was the computer wizard for MAR (Music Artists Records) during the past three years and managed to educate himself in the right places to get promoted. This time he was headed to the Corporate offices in Hollywood and was very proud of himself, becoming the fair-haired boy for the new company, Music Disc Distribution.

The Company was a major records distributor in 1974, selling all genres, including soundtracks, jazz, rock & roll, and country. Originally called Music Artists Records (MAR) and owned privately, it was then sold to a large corporate insurance company, ComAmerica, who thought it would be fun to be in the entertainment business. Little did the "bean counters" (accountants and non-music industry attorneys) know how it operated. In the end, it was again sold to ElectroDisc LTD in London, which was a much different and larger conglomerate of oil, banking, and theatres primarily throughout the U.K., with additional locations throughout the Middle East.

The young entrepreneur owner of ElectroDisc was Sir Taylor Douglas, who wanted to build a music empire and compete largely with his countryman of EMI worldwide.

He loved the Beatles and what Abbey Road Studios had accomplished and wanted to replicate it as much as he could. Business in Europe and Britain was much more civilized, and on several occasions, Sir Douglas was invited to recording sessions and events held by EMI and other labels based in the U.K.

Taylor, who was shopping for a record company and distribution, found such a bargain from ComAmerica in purchasing the company for 13 million dollars.

With the unassuming offices of MAR in Sun Valley, California that included the warehouse, sales, promotion, marketing, and operations teams that coordinated everything on the West Coast, the logo on the building wall did not indicate that it was a major force in the music industry. Nor did it's Elizabeth, New Jersey operation or the other branch offices dotted across the U.S., unless you knew about the company and where the employees worked each day.

The customer service girls on the West Coast who regularly spoke with the retailers from San Diego to Seattle were experienced phone talkers who could talk their clients into anything and did so continuously. Hence the shipments were plentiful from the unlikely, almost unknown location, off Burbank Blvd.

Not to be outdone by their counterparts in Seattle and San Francis-co, the Southern California marketing group, were the best there was in the States. It included the Radio Promotion Guys, who could get anything played on the air. Somehow even though it profited immensely from this crazy business, ComAmerica never understood it and how it all came together as a team and Company but opted to sell it off to Sir Douglas.

On this night, however, the "family" from Sun Valley let one of their own down. It was unthinkable and regrettable, especially since they appeared to be "one for all, and all for one," in almost all other functions.

Yet when Monday came around routinely, at the standard time of 8:30 AM, and the office staff began to arrive with a few exceptions, there was not one mention of Richard's party, as everyone went about their business, ready for another week.

For very few, Richards absence puzzled them, since he was normally the first one in the door to fire up the computers, to make sure that Paul was ready for the weekly updates. But other than that, no one seemed to miss him. The other three staff members who were absent sent a "where are they" comment from the others. But it was Monday, and the two Shelley's and Jeffrey were sometimes late due to the music parties they attended, so no one was the wiser for it.

Like usual and on almost any other day, Stewart, whose office was next door to the Operations Manager office, would work his inventory magic to make sure that not one item was out of stock.

Paul toiled behind the glassed-in room of computers to keep up with the data, after Richard's instructions. On occasions, Paul would come out from behind the glass wall and speak to one of the girls about a retailer, but all in all, everything was like any other day.

Carol, the boss's secretary, was in his office tidying up when the receptionist rang through to tell her that he'd be late but wanted to speak to her in his office. Sitting down, she picked up his phone and said, "Good Morning, Steve. What can I do for you? Any special needs for today?"

"Carol," Steve replied softly, "I am at Shelley Wright's apartment, and she is dead. Jeffrey and Shelley Noble found her this morning when they got back from Vegas and stopped at the apartment to pick her up for work. Jeffrey immediately called the police and then called me. They are terribly shaken by what they found!"

Steve continued, "The police have already taken down their statements, and mine, as her employer. I must tell you that it's a really horrific scene. Please do not tell anyone at the office, as I would like to discuss this tomorrow when I return. I am sure that I will be here most of the day or at the precinct. And please don't expect either Jeffrey or Noble today. I am sending them home to his place."

Carol went numb. She didn't know how to respond. Then Steve broke her trance by asking, "Are you okay with this, or do you need to go home?"

After a minute or so, Carol responded by saying, "Yeah, I am okay. Though I don't know how I am going to get through the day without telling our people, but I will try. Even Richard is out. Do you know anything about where he might be?"

"No, I haven't heard from him, so reach out and see if you can find him," replied Steve. "I will call you later tonight at home."

For a few minutes after she hung up, Carol was still in a stupor, when Stewart who was laughing at Mary spilling her coffee, came in and asked where Steve was; that he needed to go over the morning numbers with him.

Snapping out of it, Carol lied to Stewart that Steve was at Corporate and probably would not be back today and that it would have to wait till the morning. With that, Stewart turned and walked out the door towards the warehouse to speak with its manager.

Now slipping back into a trance, Carol tried to remember everything about Shelley Wright. Were her parents in town, or even alive? Where did they live? Did they already hear about their daughter's death? And what did Steve say, "a really horrific scene?" What did that mean? Trying to surmise what might have happened, she looked at the reports on Steve's desk to keep focus, but she couldn't as visions of Shelley and what it might look like at the apartment took over.

As she gazed out through the glass window towards the "bullpen," the customer sales reps were doing their jobs, without any knowledge of this devastating news. It was surrealistic.

Just then, the phone rang again on her line, which Carol was able to answer from Steve's phone. She picked up the device as her thoughts returned to the moment and said, "Hello, this is Carol, can I help you?"

It was from Richard. He said, "Carol, I am going to Cleveland to visit my Uncle, as he is in the hospital, but I will call you when I get to Ohio."

"Alright," replied Carol. Then calmly and passively said, "I will ask Paul to work time and a half while you are gone. Not to worry since you have been promoted and are moving on to a new position anyway. In the meantime, we will keep looking for your replacement, so I am sure we will be okay?"

Richard seemed aloof to Carol almost as much as Carol seemed to Richard. There were long pauses between sentences, but minutes later they ended the phone call.

Still, in a trance, Carol returned to her dilemma of maintaining some normalcy, but her mind was in chaos. Strangely Carol thought, "Were Shelley's death and Richard's impromptu leave request linked to one another?" She shook off this peculiar thought and told herself that she would have to wait to find out more from Steve that night.

By 10 AM, a couple of the sales guys stopped by, since Monday's were "quarterback" sessions with Carlo and David. Two of them asked, "where is everyone?" since there were four people out, which was abnormal. But in a disconnected response from some of the staff, the absences were of no concern and thought to be almost typical.

While a couple of the guys sat down next to their favorite girls, Mary and Jill to chat, David walked down the hall from his office, passing by the mailroom into the operations spaces and asked Carol, "Where's Steve?"

Carol looked up from the desk and again lied, "Oh, he ran over to Corporate this morning."

"Okay," replied David. "Tell him to see me later, to talk about the new female singer Lindsay Mercer and the merchandising we need to get to the retailers."

"Right," said Carol.

David Mendel was the Branch Manager for Music Disc and in charge of everything. He oversaw everyone from Carlo Gastone, the Sales Manager, and Steve Connelly, the Operations Manager, to the customer service team and warehouse operations.

David, was tough, having come up the ranks from United Artists Records over to the distribution side of MAR and now Music Disc. Though mostly a funny guy, always playing practical jokes on the staff, everyone loved him and would "go to the wall" to help him with his every need.

Carlo, the Sales Manager, on the other hand, was the "Don Juan" of the Company. Protected by the President at MAR, since he was engaged to his daughter, he was also on the prowl most of the time for a new lady friend. Apparently, his fiancé didn't mind since it never interfered in their relationship.

Comically, this held true for the salesmen and promotion guys who were loose about their relationships, even though some were married or engaged. After all, it was 1974, and the "hippy" generation lifestyle dribbled down to the everyday lives in the music business. In the words from a Crosby Stills & Nash song, "Love the one you're with" seemed to be the motto of the day, or at least in this crazy industry called "the music business."

Steve, who was the Operations Manager, ran the office like a machine to make sure that inventory and merchandising supplies were on hand and ready to roll out for any artist and retailer that needed it. And his staff loved him because he was tough and demanding yet protective and willing to lend a hand always.

The annual income for the Company was about twenty million dollars a year, with artists and labels coming and going. Sometimes you'd have the biggest or hottest name on the label only to be sued and lose that artist to Warner's or Columbia, or some other label, in a short time.

There is a story of an artist manager jumping on a President's desk wielding a gun and threatening the President if the artist (name withheld) wasn't let out of his contract.

Some noted and major record companies came and went through mergers and bankruptcies in droves. Salespeople and other staff members changed jobs in as little as two years because of management. And marriages and divorces took their tolls just as fast.

For anyone to be part of this rollercoaster ride, they experienced something unique in this professional world. Major Corporate companies like ComAmerica, or Mobil Oil or the Ford Motor Company, did not, nor could understand how this business operated on a consignment basis to record retailers, with returns and payola taking place regularly. Yet, Wall Street conversely loved these wacky type mogul-run companies, and the "Big Money" it could generate. It was either a hit or miss, and some companies lost everything as either a startup or as a well-established record company, in a very short time.

Royalties to artists and advances were just as much as a deterrent as it was a sign of profitability. One-hit wonders populated much of the industry, who ended up washing the cars for the same people who signed them to a contract. Unfortunately, most artists signed seven-year contracts that tied them to a heavy commitment with a label.

Many artists would blow an advance of $250,000 or greater and have no additional income unless they were lucky enough to tour for the remainder of their contract. Sometimes called a business for the insane, or insane asylum, one such record label was actually called Asylum...

The Music Disc Murder
Chapter 2

Two years prior, in 1972, Shelley Wright met Shelley Noble at-tending UCLA's, The Actors Workshop. They were both 22 years old, having gone to Hollywood High School at the same time, but never knew each other, as they traveled with different crowds and held different jobs after school. Wright came from a more than a wealthy white family who lived in Beverly Hills.

Noble came from a mulatto San Fernando farm family, who sold their property and became rich in comparison to many of their neighbors. They then moved to a sensible house on Fountain in Los Angeles.

Noble's Dad found a job and worked for the Agriculture Department of Los Angeles County, while Wright's family came from old Hollywood Movie money, who moved about the rich and famous.

Shortly after their meeting each other and attending classes together, they decided to leave the safety of their parents' homes and branch out on their own, moving in together to an apartment on Cherokee. It was a typical old Spanish type home that dotted the skyline of the LA Hollywood neighborhoods. Usually separated into two or three apartment complexes, the two Shelley's lived in one of these apartment homes.

The girls lucked out since this was one of the few available two-bedroom apartments on the block. The owner and another older couple completed the triad in the complex who lived there for fifteen years each.

Unquestionably, the two Shelley's were almost alike with jet black hair, small pointed noses, and stood five feet five inches tall. The exception was that Wright had green eyes and pale skin, while Noble was exotic looking with blue eyes and tan, almost brown skin. But in the dark, they looked almost the same, except that Noble sported a small dolphin tattoo on her right ankle that was a sign of independence against her parents as she grew up in the "Valley."

It was after the family had taken a trip to Sea World in San Diego that she fought with her Mom and Dad about getting a tattoo, and they finally agreed on the non-obtrusive design.

While at The Workshop, they met Jeffrey Ashton and Jimmy Columbo. Ashton lived alone off Highland and was particularly fond of his many boyfriends who frequented The Troubadour on Santa Monica in West Hollywood.

Jeffrey and Ashton were instrumental in telling the girls that they worked at Music Disc, (at that time called MAR). They inform the two Shelley's that the company was looking for additional employees. Ashton told them that he would let them know when the Sun Valley location would be holding interviews, and they should consider applying. Giving Ashton their phone number, it was too long before he called them with the particular dates for the interview.

The hiring women at MAR were Ruth, who also controlled the returns and accounting and of course, Carol, Steve's assistant/secretary.

After the interview, they agreed that the two Shelley's would be beneficial in helping the company maintain it's youthfulness appeal, especially with the girl's good looks and talkative personalities. Hired on the spot, they were asked to start in two days.

As a side note, Ruth and Carol were like having another "Mom," as they were always looking out for the "Kids" they employed.

During her initial hiring, Noble told the women that she was a paid extra at Twentieth Century Studios and seemed to be making her way up the ladder in the movie business.

Both women told Noble that it wasn't a deal-breaker since MAR, aka Music Disc, thought this was a brilliant connection and sought to use her involvement to their benefit. So, the company didn't mind sharing her on the days she was required to be on-site for a shoot.

Even after ElectroDisc purchased the company, Sir Douglas encouraged Noble to continue her involvement in the movie business.

As stated, the girls could have passed for sisters.

Shelley Wright looked like a combination of Ava Gardner and Jacqueline Bisset, and Noble looked a little like Diahann Carroll with Bisset's facial cheekbone features.

The two girls were quite the lookers that dated many different types, who wined and dined them regularly.

The suitors that sometimes called on the young women at their respective parent's homes in Beverly Hills and Hollywood sought to launch their relationships into those affluent families.

Those who dated Wright, knew all too well what money there was behind Shelley. Her Dad was the President of an animation studio that rivaled Disney.

He'd gotten into the business as a child working with his father, who was an animator. Eventually, his Father took over the independent company of Cartoon Frontier and created several well-known characters that became the opening cartoons for theaters across America. When his father passed away, Brad Wright assumed control and made it more profitable than when his father was alive.

Shelley Wright was set for life, even if she never worked a day in her life. But raised as an independent type, Wright opted to pursue her own dreams and only went to her Dad for help, when times were tough, which was seldom.

Nobel, with her unique beauty, became a skilled actress that continued to improve her craft at The Workshop. In time, she climbed out of being an extra and became a stand-in for several actresses, and it appeared that it was just a matter of time before some director or producer would have hired her as the leading lady.

Jimmy, who was amazed by Noble's natural beauty, really wanted her, but she was aloof and non-responsive to his boyish immature charm.

As a struggling drummer, and the younger brother of Bobby Columbo, a sales rep at MAR, he went through life casually, with no plans except to play in a rock and roll band. Somehow, he was able to make a living by working unusual jobs that came from a variety of sources and allowed him the freedom that he nurtured.

Jimmy was a person never concerned where his next paycheck was coming from, nor how much. He hung around the Sun Valley offices and was given odd jobs, and so he was always invited to and normally attended the same functions as his brother Bobby.

Off Sunset Blvd on Larrabee, Jimmy, Bobby, along with his wife Evie, lived in a large house right up the street from The Whiskey. One of the most famous clubs in LA.

Usually two or three times a week, Jimmy was hired to sit in at one of the local rock & roll clubs, either because he was connected to MAR or because of his brother working there. Or so it was stated by more than one business owner and musician, "Jimmy was only hired because of his connections since he was not a very good drummer, only adequate."

However, one night, when Billy Joel opened for Ballin' Jack, at the Troubadour their drummer was sick. So, Jimmy was called in and was ready and willing and performed gallantly for the band.

The band, Ballin' Jack's only hit came in 1970 was called "Super Highway." It was also one of the few times that Jimmy played for a star.

Several months after they met at The Workshop, Shelley Wright and Jimmy began to date, even though he was more interested in Noble at the start. It was a normal twenties, something romance, where the attention was in parties, concerts, drinking, some drugs, and of course, much sex. Sex was very prevalent throughout the '70s. Hookups occurred in clubs, restaurants, and the house parties that took place.

Ironically the first time that Jimmy asked Wright out on a date, she refused.

She told him, "I am not interested in anyone who is a musician, nor anyone who has charted out their life. I am strictly looking for a man who is permanent and secure, though if you don't mind hanging around, that would be enjoyable!"

Even though Jimmy was taken by her charm, in spite of Noble's unique looks, he felt that it was the only way of making his inroads with either girl and agreed by saying, "Sure whatever you want, I'll do."

Unbeknownst to Jimmy, and not to be left behind, Noble had begun to date an actor at the same time.

Nathan Brown was a remarkably handsome man that imitated the flair and style of Harry Belafonte, and because there were so few outstanding black actors, he managed to find several supporting roles and was being hired by directors because of his panache. The unfortunate thing about Nathan Brown was that he fancied himself a ladies' man, and it didn't much matter whether the woman was black or white; he was always on the hunt. The problem is that he lost out on several movie and tv roles because of his philandering.

All the while, Noble didn't mind his unfaithfulness, because her main goal was acting, and while she worked at MAR and Music Disc, she had fallen for and become Carlo's permanent girlfriend.

Unluckily, Noble's steady, Nathan Brown, was the hapless romantic and initially wanted to date Shelley Wright, but she didn't find him exciting enough, perhaps because of his color, though he never knew the real reason. Thus, Nathan almost allowed himself to become obsessed with Shelley.

Nathan sometimes visualized making love to Shelley when he was in bed with Noble. It was a quandary that was foreign to Nathan.

Oddly, although Shelley and Jimmy seemed to be going strong, there was way too much tension caused by Jimmy's jealousy, as the year went by.

Shelley Wright went on to become the number one customer service rep for MAR/Music Disc in 1974, calling on all the best retail buyers, including all Southern California Tower Records and Licorice Pizza stores.

During an event to help celebrate Shelley's success, held in the Sun Valley offices, a cake was served, and most of the staff attended and had a good time that day. Regrettably, Jimmy had been working in the warehouse at the same time, loading record boxes for a shipment, and missed the whole event.

Unexpectedly, a couple of the warehouse guys who had been in the office spaces made it known to Jimmy that his brother Bobby had been standing behind Shelley with his hands on her shoulders.

The warehouse guys joked and smiled at Jimmy, telling him that his brother was moving in on his girlfriend. This may have been overstated, but this infuriated Jimmy, who started throwing boxes up into the truck when the warehouse manager yelled at him to stop.

That evening when he got home, he walked right up to Shelley as she stood up to greet him, and he slapped her face and started yelling at her. "How dare you treat me like that and not even acknowledge me and allow my brother to hold you. I didn't know about the party that was in your honor!"

Shelley tried to defend herself and said, "Jimmy, I knew nothing about it until Steve rounded up everyone, and there was cake brought in by David and Carlo. Why are you blaming me for this?"

Jimmy started yelling again and blurted out, "Because you are always recognized, and I am not. I am just the drummer, and I am tired of it."

Shelley tried to soothe Jimmy's ego by saying, "Try out for some movie parts, go with Noble on auditions or sign up with the union to try and get more work and recognition as a drummer."

Jimmy would listen to none of it and stormed out of the door, leaving Shelley in tears.

That night it wasn't until 2:30 AM that Jimmy returned home, drunk, and stumbled to the couch where he slept.

Shelley had once more cried herself to sleep and promised herself that she was going to get out of her relationship with Jimmy because she was tired of his abuse.

As the eighth month passed by since her first encounter with Bobby, Shelley was becoming more infatuated with him, as he was with her, continuing to flirt with each other, particularly when he came to the office.

Bobby's attitude, manners, and cologne were making her giddy around him. And though a much older man, he was more mature and well established than most of the other guys she dated. Yes, she knew he was married to Evie, but it seemed not to matter as they were both smitten and couldn't get enough of each other.

As Shelley was to learn that Bobby's marriage was already on the rocks, on more than one occasion, Evie told Bobby, "I am off to New York as usual, but may find myself going to London if ABD needs me."

To which, Bobby, the seasoned traveler, would always say, "Okay, have a good trip, and I'll see you when you return."

Evie was an up and coming top executive in her own right that became the highest positioned marketing person for ABD Records (American, Broadway, and Downtown). ABD's main offices were in New York at the affectionate location called "The Dark Pillar," on 56th St, with Branch offices in Dallas, San Francisco, Chicago, Los Angeles, and a satellite office at Apple Records in London.

Evie traveled much of the time, and sometimes she and Bobby would only see each other once a month. With all the travel that they both did, the house rarely was ever occupied by more than two people at any given time.

Without Bobby's knowledge, Evie had fallen for Sir Taylor Douglas since meeting him in Jamaica on a record company event that started a merger of ABD with ElectroDisc, which led to the purchase of MAR.

Sir Douglas had taken to Evie, and she was very captivated by his style and flair. It wasn't long before they were hiding their affair and spending time together in London, New York, and other out of the way places.

Back in the States, as time passed, when Bobby came to the Sun Valley office with that big smile on his face, he would grab the chair that was next to Ruth and drag it to where Shelley sat. There the two of them would flirt and chat it up like children until he had to meet with Carlo or if Steve chased him out of the office.

Noble, busily with her other career, on many occasions, would hand out free movie passes for a yet to be released movie. Usually, she would drop by MAR and Music Disc to hand them out to anyone who would want to attend, and this included Jimmy.

Several times, Jimmy ended up with Noble after the screenings and would try and hustle her into sleeping with him, even though he was dating Wright. But Noble knew better and declined his persistent offers. Then he'd beg Noble not discuss it or mention it to anyone, including Shelley.

In reverse, Nathan was trying desperately to sleep with Shelley. One night after bedding down with Noble, he crept into Shelley's room to persuade her to allow him to make love to her. He said, "You don't have to do anything; just let me love you."

Shelley became panicked and quietly dismissed Nathan by saying, "If you ever try this again, I will tell Noble," as she ushered him out of her room, locking the door behind him.

Like other record companies, Music Disc had its rumor mill that somehow swirled around Noble's reputation. She was the girl that "took care of the sales team." However, there was no truth to it.

Jimmy, as it turned out, had started it because of Noble's resistance to his single-mindedness of sleeping with him and wanted to get back at her.

Noble, only on rare occasions, would attend a function with Nathan since she was, after all, the number one girlfriend of Carlo.

Though Nobel spent time almost every day locked in Carlo's office, there were only a few comments ever made by David, whose office was next door.

Engaged, Carlo used Noble for his gratification, and she didn't mind. And in fact, she cherished her time with Carlo, and that was anytime and anywhere and wouldn't have it any other way.

One night at Stephen Bishop's introduction at Capitol Records Studios, Bobby invited the entire MAR/MD staff, including his brother Jimmy, the two Shelley's, and Jeffrey.

Unfortunately, Jimmy had a gig that night at Disneyland and couldn't make it. Even though he knew about the event, he told Shelley and Bobby to have a good time, though, in his heart, he didn't mean it.

During that night, there was more giggling and handholding by Bobby and Shelley to the point that Noble gently chimed in, saying, "Okay, you two love birds, enough. Everyone is already attached and spoken for if you know what I mean."

When Bobby finally drove Shelley home at 1:30 in the morning, she got home in the nick of time right before Jimmy drove his car up the driveway at 1:45 AM.

As Shelley was getting ready for bed, coming out of the bathroom, Jimmy knew that something was up.

Shelley said, "Hi, how was your evening? Mine was a blast at the studio. All of us hung out until your brother drove me home a little while ago."

Jimmy seething, looked at her with his steel-blue eyes, and said, "How is my brother? Is he still trying to steal my girl?"

Shelley laughed and replied, "No, we just had a good time together along with everyone else."

Jimmy refused to believe her and told her goodnight and went into the living room where he slept on the couch.

The other girls from Music Disc, who had steady boyfriends, would, on occasion, hit the sack with musicians or other industry guys. Strangely enough, this group of misfits all seemed to work and play together no matter what.

During countless nights on Sunset at the famed restaurant Carlos and Charlie's, many of the movie industry celebrities hung out. C&C was the who's who club to showcase artists from any label since the mix of people included industry, press, actors, and actresses alike.

There was a rule for anyone in attendance to give the label A&R and other label executives presenting an artist or band either a thumbs up or thumbs down for a performance. It was a way to empower the audience in the future of an act or band. Sometimes it did an act or even broke it. (Several A&R guys lost their jobs over signing an act who did not get a thumbs up on their first night).

Hence the girls from the office almost always found themselves there till closing and going home with someone other than their boyfriends.

The Music Disc Murder
Chapter 3

Around three years before the two Shelley's began working at MAR/Music Disc, Richard Graydon started his new job as the computer tech. The computer system that ComAmerica incorporated into MAR at the time was a smaller model called the IBM RPG III. Richard, employed by ComAmerica, jumped at the opportunity to get into the record business by moving over to the newly purchased company.

ComAmerica, the top insurance company in the U.S., provided daily reports to MAR management to review sales and expenses to keep the company on target and not out of whack.

Generally, there was nothing to worry about, but ComAmerica was created with "accountants," and money guys and so management was always worried about the bottom line, particularly with the purchase of a wild bronco type business in the entertainment field. (The "Record guys" hated the accountants, they just wanted to make deals, party and spend money doing so.)

With Richard, he was the only tech, working a four-day week, ten hours a day. So after validating Richard's position after numerous battles with ComAmerica, Steve Connelly and David at MAR were finally permitted to hire another computer person to run two full shifts.

However, before this happened and shortly after Shelley Wright was hired, Richard immediately fell in love with her. Shelley thought that Richard was sweet but was not attracted to him at all.

This was a bit unfair, and some might say pathetic because Shelley asked Richard all the time to help her with something, and he was all too willing for any chance to do just that.

Almost from the very start, Richard would leave something on Shelley's desk, though never acknowledging that it was from him. For weeks on end, he left offerings of fruit or candy, and when Shelley went to Carol to complain, no one did anything about it and just laughed it off.

"You have a secret admirer" was the answer from almost everyone who would chuckle and gossip about who it might be since the salesmen would come and go in the office. Eventually, it stopped right before Richard was moved to the late afternoon and evening shift.

For a while, Richard did nothing, since he only saw her for about an hour each afternoon. But there were company parties yet to come in which Richard and Shelley would attend. And even though he would have his moments of standing or sitting in the same area as she, his opportunities of conversing with Shelley seemed always to be interrupted. There was constantly someone else vying for her attention, and she was naïve to think that Richard was not one of them.

Once at the famous LA club, "Whiskey" for one of MAR's album release events, Richard was forced right up against her, as the crowd on the dancefloor squeezed its way from the front doors to the stage.

He could smell her perfume permeating his senses, almost making him delirious. He tried talking to her only to be drummed out by the rock and roll on the stage.

She sensed that he was saying something to her, but couldn't understand and motioned that she was leaving with Noble. It seemed that outside the office, there was never any time for him. Crushed, Richard knew his chance slipped away in the blaring sounds of the night.

There were other events in which he was able to initiate a shy conversation with Shelley, but as usual, either Noble seemed to be protecting her, or someone else would stop by and draw her away from him to another place or into another discussion.

Following these events, Richard would usually go home and drink himself to sleep, however not before breaking something in his apartment in anguish.

The rage sometimes was beyond his control, and yet in the mornings, he would vow to have his day with her. He constantly dreamt of that first kiss, making love and his wedding day with Shelley. This was his goal, no matter what, and who was in his way.

It was several months later on the night shift, and after attending numerous functions as a group from the Sun Valley office that Richard once again began leaving little gifts on Shelley's desk.

The one that broke the camel's back was a small Tiffany box that she opened to see a necklace and a note that read, "To be Engraved Later."

Shelley looked around the office and saw that everyone was busy either on the phone or working on something on their desk and paid no attention to her. With that, she opened her top right-hand drawer and threw the box inside and slammed it shut.

She was furious that she didn't know who was doing this and a little afraid, since everyone seemed so normal and not involved. So, Shelley decided for the moment to just let it go, and that maybe whoever was obsessed with her would stop leaving these things on her desk.

When another week went by, Shelley began telling Jeffrey and Noble everything and that she thought it was a bit creepy since it started when she originally was hired, then stopped and then restarted.

Jeffrey, in his sassy jibe, said, "Oh Shell, it's someone who wants to be your boyfriend. I wouldn't worry about that girl."

However, Noble cautiously added a small warning to Jeffrey's comment, "Yeah, okay, but it would be nice to know who thought of you this way?"

Shelley agreed and told Noble that she was going to ask everyone she knew, in and out of the office, because it made her feel uneasy, and for the first time, she felt a bit scared.

Noble asked Wright, "Should we hire a private investigator to find out who is doing this?"

Wright replied, "No, I will find out myself."

In the lunchroom a few days later, Jeffrey smugly said, "I'll protect you, as will Noble. We won't let anything happen to you. Right Noble?" Noble nodded and said, "I will help you find out who this is and kick him in, you know what!"

Before either of them could do anything, Richard heard the rumblings and decided that he needed to leave a note apologizing and asked if he could meet Shelley outside of the office, since he hadn't meant to frighten or scare her.

Upon finding the note on her desk, Shelley immediately walked to Steve's office and complained that she already was involved with a boyfriend and was not interested in pursuing anything with Richard.

Shelley also told Steve how long it had been going on.

She then demanded that Steve speak with Richard to stop this harassment.

With that, Steve told Shelley that he would take care of the situation that day.

Knowing this could be trouble not just for Shelley but for the company, Steve asked Carol to come into his office to discuss this strange conduct by Richard since he never displayed this type of behavior before to anyone.

Even though Shelley told Noble what happened, she never mentioned it to Jeffrey, but he knew something was in that note which had upset Shelley very much.

Wanting to help protect Shelley, as he did always, he decided that he would convince Noble to let him know what had transpired.

That afternoon, Shelley requested that she be allowed to go home early and not be there to confront Richard.

Approved, Carol told her no problem, and Shelley left right after lunch.

Jeffrey was bound and determined to find out and took Noble and Shelley to a Mexican restaurant down the street in hopes of getting the lowdown. But neither of the girls would speak about it and only joked that it was a "girl thing."

Around four, Richard came in to begin work, but Steve asked Paul to stand by in case he might have to work a double shift.

Arriving on time, Richard was all smiles and "hello's" to everyone. But he noticed that Shelley was not at her desk, and a small frown crept unto his face as he walked into the glassed-in room, where Paul was threading a tape on the computer.

Paul said, "Hey, Steve wants to chat with you before you start your day."

Putting his bag down, Richard looked at Paul and said, "Do you know why?"

Paul casually responded by saying. "Nope, don't know, not sure. He didn't say anything to me."

With that, Richard walked towards Steve's office, where Carol told him to go in and wait for him, as he was with David, the Branch Manager.

Returning to his office, Steve closed the door and sat down. He looked at Richard, who was about to say something and stopped him.

"Richard," Steve said, "You have freaked Shelley out, and you need to stop. She has a boyfriend, and whatever you are feeling for her, you need to let it go. She is not interested. You do understand, right?"

Richard was shocked that Steve now knew what was going on between him and Shelley. He apologized profusely to him, then said, "I promise you that it would never happen again. I only felt that I might have a chance with her since she was having issues with Jimmy as he heard, and that is why he kept on soliciting for her attention."

Steve looked at Richard and said, "Let it alone. In fact, for the next week or so, come in later, around 5:30, after the staff has gone to let this thing blow over.

Richard told Steve that he would do as he was asked.

After work that night, though, Richard couldn't let well enough alone.

Richard, in his stubborn approach, drove by Shelley's apartment several times, wondering if he should knock on her door and apologize.

He knew what Steve said, but he thought that if he ever was going to get another chance, he needed to apologize to her in person.

After the third time driving by, the lights in the apartment were turned off, and Richard went home and drank himself to sleep.

The following night he repeated his actions and did nothing except think about Shelley and how to redeem himself and wait till the lights went out to make sure she was safe.

On the third night, he went to the Bombay Bar on Sunset after repeating his actions for the past two nights and found a young woman who was willing to listen to Richard's sad story. She then invited him back to her apartment, and when he got to the front door of her place, he was held up by the woman's pimp.

Fortunately for Richard, he only had $100.00 on him that night and handed it over to the guy. Then the two of them left him standing there, and he walked back to his car to find that he had a flat. It was turning into a typical night for Richard.

When he got himself home, it was almost 4 AM.

After a few drinks, he crashed out on the couch and hoped that a new day would bring him much better luck.

The Music Disc Murder
Chapter 4

At 36 years of age, Jeffrey was much older than most
of the other staff members except for management,
at MAR/Music Disc.

His younger guy friends considered Jeffrey the "queen
bee" of Hollywood.

Born an orphan, he lucked out living in Buffalo, where
a wealthy couple that couldn't have children adopted
a boy and a girl.

The girl Elizabeth called Elsie, and Jeffrey grew up in
the comforts of old money from the textile mills, that
belonged to the Ashton Family.

Originally from Cornwall, the Ashton family had
migrated to America in 1890 as the agricultural
depression hit England. In Buffalo, they were
fortunate enough to help establish the mills which
they ultimately ended up owning.

The two children were the delight to their parents and
to the community where they lived. At a time when
the "gay" life was unspoken and tucked away in a
closet, Jeffrey was free to move about the high
society in East Aurora, together with his sister.

As good kids, they sang and danced their way
through private schools and went to Canisius, which
was founded in the 1800s by Je-suits from Germany.

The school began with one building in downtown Buffalo. Today it was larger than life with it's complex in the suburbs of Buffalo and was funded almost entirely by the Ashtons.

The unfortunate part of Jeffrey's life came when he was 20, and his adoptive parents called him into the parlor to have a family meeting.

They informed him that his birth father had recently died in prison and that his birth mother passed away when he was only three.

Jeffrey seemed uncertain about this new knowledge and what it might shed on his life since his Dad had been a criminal.

Initially, he wanted to know the circumstances of the why, what, and where, but the Ashtons only told him that his father, Benjamin, had been behind bars for crimes not fitting for a respectable family.

In time, Jeffrey seemed to bury this and went about his business, forgetting about his Dad, and never brought it up again. In this regard, he remained very much like an Ashton, keeping his real feelings buried.

Elsie's parents, as it turned out, passed away naturally, or so she was told, and no one ever heard anything else about them. Still, it was believed that they died in an auto accident when she was only a baby.

Elsie was two years younger than Jeffrey, so there was always the big brother protection for her at school and any other place they went.

Jeffrey left Buffalo after graduation with a degree in Fashion, which was added to the curriculum since it wasn't offered.

Noteworthy was that his parent's influence and ability had much more control over the school in those days than anyone else in the community.

The Ashtons were the city's number one Catholic family and contributed heavily to the expansion of the University, so his degree included English and Theatre, as secondary disciplines.

Jeffrey moved around for a few years dabbling in Chicago Theatre, then in San Francisco, before ending up in West Hollywood.

A monthly trust fund kept him well funded in his choice of large deco apartments, antique cars, and outlandish clothes.

Between the money received and his daytime job, it allowed him to maintain the lifestyle he loved.

Regrettably, his adoptive parents had passed away, and he missed them terribly.

Sometimes he and his sister would get together in Buffalo, where she remained and married an attorney who also went to Canisius and maintained his

practice. Though distant from each other, they pre-
served a close bond not easily broken.

When Steve hired Jeffrey, it was done as a favor for
Father Michael Patrick, the Professor of Media at
Canisius.

Father Patrick was originally the Pastor at St. Charles
Borromeo in North Hollywood, where Steve and
Jordan were married and attended church.

Steve never regretted doing this favor, because
Jeffrey turned out to be an asset since he was well-
liked within the Company, and by his other record
business associates.

The Music Disc Murder
Chapter 5

In Los Angeles, the "sweet-set," as the two Shelley's
and Jeffrey were often referred to, made the rounds
of the famous and infamous West Hollywood clubs
and Hollywood parties.

Sometimes Noble or Wright would attend these by
themselves because of Noble's busy life with her own
invitations and onsite movie roles and parts.

Interesting enough, a few times, the girls decided to
go as each other, to no one's knowledge. It was
initially done on a whim but proved to be beneficial a
couple of times when neither one of them wanted to
go to the event they were scheduled to attend.

Invited by many rock and rollers living in Laurel
Canyon, the "sweet-set" could do no wrong. Though
sometimes arriving a little late to work in the
mornings, the Management in Sun Valley and Hollywood looked the other way. The gang of three
became an important marketing team and secret A&R
scouts for Music Disc while hanging out with the rest
of the record business execs and artists, by hobnob-
bing.

During one of Jeffrey's house parties, many record
industry people, along with the Sun Valley staff, came
by, including Carlo, David, and most of the sales and
promotional teams.

On a particular evening, Evie was in town and also came by for some fun, bringing with her a few friends from her own label group.

Even though he technically lived alone, Jeffrey's apartment was a large four-bedroom, three-bath second-story flat, in a massive complex, with a balcony that extended over the two-car garage and looked out towards Beverly Hills and Century City.

On any full moon or star covered cool evening, the night lights of the street would follow its way to the bottom of Santa Monica Boulevard, where you could see the ocean shimmering.

On that night, two incidents were most troubling to those in attendance.

Richard, as usual, unfortunately, got extremely drunk and started flirting with Noble, though in his mind, he thought it was Shelley. He was barely holding himself up against the wall, slurring his words and challenged a few of the guys to a fight, including Jimmy, who was almost as drunk as Richard.

Though Jimmy paid no attention to whatever Richard was saying, he continued to focus his interest on a young woman in the furthest corner of the living room without much notice of anyone else.

Babbling that several guys were cutting in on his turf, Richard insisted that he loved Shelley and was willing to die for her. The drunkenness didn't bother anyone, but upon hearing this loud interchange going on, Shelley and other guests began to feel uneasy as the night wore on. Noble then moved away from Richard as he bantered on by himself.

Odd that when they were both sober, Jimmy looked more like Richard's brother than Bobby, as they both stood five feet ten, with blue eyes and sandy color hair. Sensing another blow out by Richard, a salesman by the name of Ronnie, along with Bobby, came to Shelley's rescue, which raised an eyebrow or two, particularly after Bobby took Shelley outside onto the balcony.

Richard's two buddies from work, Stewart and Paul, were stoned and paid no attention as they were munching down chips and dip and laughed at Richard.

Meanwhile, Ronnie escorted Richard outside to a cab that had been called by Jeffrey. Then Ronnie told the driver where to take him and gave the cabbie money for the trip.

Standing at the far end of the balcony, under an almost full moon, Bobby held Shelley. He spoke to her tenderly, saying that everything was going to be alright, while Evie looked on from the living room of what was taking place.

Shelley felt protected and safe, looking into Bobby's eyes. A spark lit up like a rocket between the two of them, and it was apparent even to Evie at that distance that a moment of guiltless intimacy was going on, even if they didn't know it at the time.

Jimmy was too drunk to see anything on the balcony, so he never knew that his brother was falling in love with Shelley.

Noble, who was chatting with Carlo, saw what was happening outside on the balcony and excused herself. She decided to interrupt whatever was going on, or else there would be more problems, especially with Evie.

On her way out to the balcony, Noble passed by Evie and said aloud, "Oh, there you are. Can we go now? I am very tired?"

With that, the moment was interrupted between Bobby and Shelley, and the girls left the party without saying much except, "Goodnight, thank you, see you all later."

Jeffrey's main boyfriend, who was speaking with Evie when all this was taking place, was drunk too and perhaps should have kept his mouth shut.

Nevertheless, he said to Shelley and Noble as they walked out, "You no good bitches, someone should take care of you!"

It probably didn't mean what it sounded like, but later that night, Jeffrey was so pissed at his friend that he kicked him out of the apartment and told him never to come back. After all, Jeffrey was very close to the girls, and no one was allowed to speak to or act like that towards them.

As George was leaving, everyone heard, "I'll show you, you bastard!" then slammed the door shut.

Though Jeffrey just shrugged his shoulders and made a comment that "boys will be boys," a rumbling amongst the guests suggested that it could be otherwise.

No one it seemed would ever have suspected his friend of murder, but when the cops heard the story, they began to snoop into George Hill's life. What they found twisted the possible events of Shelley's death.

Nobel driving home to their apartment, scolded Shelley. She told Shelley that her flirtation with Bobby would lead to his divorce from Evie.

But Shelley responded by telling her that they were already on their way to separating and that she would not be responsible for their marriage breaking apart and that it was way too late because she was already in love with him.

Though there was not much else said during the rest of the party, on the way home, Evie and Bobby engaged in a fight about the evening. By the time they arrived at their door, neither of them were talking, and Bobby slept on the couch, while Evie slept in their bedroom.

Someplace else, in another part of the LA Basin, as Richard awoke the next day, he didn't know how he got home.

Getting up off the bed, he staggered to the bathroom and looked into the mirror. Agonized, he took his right hand and broke the medicine cabinet, as the glass shattered into the palm of his hand.

He cursed himself for being a jerk and knew that he was driving himself further away than nearer to Shelley. He knew he needed to control himself, or else something terrible might happen.

After cleaning up the mess and wrapping his hand in a towel, he called for a cab to take him back to where his car was at Jeffrey's before heading to the North Hollywood Medical emergency room.

As he got out of the cab, he looked at the towel. It was now bloodstained. Yep, he knew he needed stitches desperately for that hand.

The Music Disc Murder
Chapter 6

The shared apartment of Wright and Noble was a single-story Spanish style home that had been transformed into three spacious apartments.

The courtyard included a fountain, small garden with hedges, driveway, a three-car garage, and a round-about for easy visiting, parking, and exiting.

The open apartment had two bedrooms, two bathrooms, a dining room and a chef's dream kitchen with an island for preparation of food.

Each room, including the large living room, had a ceiling fan and floor to ceiling windows. There was no air conditioning, but the front and rear of the house had large over-grown palm and pine trees that kept the house cool from the LA sun.

As Sergeant Murphy drilled Steve about Shelley, he was almost threatening in his approach.

"Mr. Connelly, what do you know about what happened here? Who are you to the deceased? Were you her lover? Do you have a key to the apartment? And so on..."

Murphy seemed to go on and on with many other questions that made Steve feel guilty and uneasy.

By the time that Lieutenant Long arrived, he could see how Murphy's accusations were affecting Steve and told the Sergeant to "throttle back."

The Lieutenant then apologized to Steve, but by then, he was too traumatized to shed the feelings of guilt. Long, however, persuaded Steve to tell him what he did know and kept it civil.

In the apartment and positioned obscenely, the police found Shelley's body naked except for a see-through lingerie robe. It appeared that it was an afterthought and just thrown over the top of her.

Laying face-up on the couch, it appeared her neck was broken, according to the police. While one leg was on the floor and the other one rested slightly bent over a pillow.

A small trail of blood seemed to have started in the bedroom where the initial confrontation probably took place, according to Murphy.

There were handprint marks still left around her neck with some bruising on her left cheek, along with traces of blood that had trickled from her nose and mouth.

The police surmised she must have known who was in the room with her since the lock on the door was not broken, nor were there any broken windows.

On her bed in disarray, the pillows and rumpled satin sheets appeared they were used for more than sleeping. And though there seemed to be some blood spots, the blood on the floor told the Sergeant that the killing took place right after what may have happened on the bed.

With no suicide note or apparent struggle, the cops immediately ruled it as a homicide and asked Steve to go with them to the station, in case he could fill in anything missing in this unusual case.

Upon ending the initial investigation, the police told Noble that she would have to find some other place to stay since the apartment and premises was now a crime scene.

Jeffrey offered up his place, and Noble asked if she could take anything of hers and was told "no," not until they dusted for fingerprints and went from room to room to see if there was any additional information that they could obtain.

Mrs. Alvarez, the retired owner of the complex, who also lived in one of the apartments, told the police that the Shelley's were very good tenants, paid their rent on time, and never throw any wild parties. She did mention that there were a few different men that frequented the girl's apartment at times, but oddly enough, it was always the same men.

Mr. and Mrs. Pope were long-time tenants, and both worked at CBS Television City on Beverly Boulevard. He was a set designer, and she worked in publicity. With no children of their own, they would invite the two Shelley's over for meals on numerous occasions.

The Popes had nothing bad to say about either of the girls.

Neither of the other residents was at home during the time of Shelley's death. Mrs. Alvarez was visiting her daughter, where she spent the night returning early that morning. And the Pope's were in San Diego until they returned in the morning to go to work.

The police did not have much to go on, but they brought in the dogs and their "Crime Scene Investigation" team to go through the apartment and gather up what evidence they could find and try to figure out who the other person was with Shelley.

Perplexed, the police spoke to the neighbors to make sure they did not miss any leads. In doing so, the older woman who lived across the street told the police that she remembered seeing a man coming out of the apartment when she took her dog out for a very late walk.

They asked her if she thought she could recognize him, and she told them "no" since it was dark. However, she assumed that his hair was fair, light color, and was maybe six feet tall, from the lights shining off the street lamps. With that, they thought they had gotten enough and called it a day.

By the time Steve returned home that evening, it was nearly 11 PM. Regrettably, he had sat most of his time in the Lieutenant's office without adding any additional information into the investigation.

Nonetheless, the cops felt that he needed to be there just in case.

His wife, Jordan, was still up and waiting for him and rushed to his arms when he came through the door.

The Connelly's lived in an apartment complex on Balboa Blvd., in Encino, where the world seemed calm and peaceful. But the day's events were not anything like that.

Steve retold what he knew to Jordan, as she began to sob. Neither of them had ever encountered such a ghastly thing, and all Steve could visualize was the image of Shelley, laying on the couch, as if thrown there like a piece of litter. Her body cruelly placed and lifeless.

Carol, who went through the entire day without hearing back from Steve, was frantic beyond belief. She unrelentingly called Jordan almost every half hour to see if he'd gotten home.

Jordan finally asked, "What the hell happened that you are calling so much." With that, Carol blurted out to Jordan what Steve told her. They both then cried for what seemed to be an hour.

After Steve recounted the day, Jordan said, "You need to call Carol and give her the latest update. She has been hysterical all day."

Steve did as she asked.

In relating what they found at Shelley's and what the police thought, Carol was baffled by it all. The timing of Richard taking off for Cleveland and Shelley's murder seemed to be both a bit ironic.

Though Steve did not know it at the time of his statements to the police, he told Carol that he would notify the cops in the morning, of Richard's request, just in case there was any connection.

As the torrential rain pelted the Los Angeles basin the following morning, Steve gathered everyone inside Music Disc to deliver the heartbreaking news, without the gruesome details.

Gasps and tears surrounded the room as he told all what had happened and what the police findings were to date.

Absent that morning was Bobby, who did not hear the news that everyone else did.

When Steve was done telling everyone the news, Carlo asked if he knew where Noble was.

Steve told him that both she and Jeffrey were told to stay home, and that Noble spent the night at his place.

David offered his assistance to anyone if they needed it, and the business at Music Disc was shut down for the day as David told every-one to pack up and go home.

Steve tried calling the main office to inform them of the tragic news; however, management was in seclusion for meetings all day to discuss the merger into ElectroDisc.

Thus no one knew what grief had befallen the company.

While Noble told Shelley to watch out what she was doing, on more than one occasion, her words seemed to fall on deaf ears.

Shelley, as it turned out, was very much open in her love interests with several guys than Noble when it came to relationships.

Shelley, being the wild child of the two, was the first one to lose her virginity in high school, while Noble waited till she was in college and then only with one boyfriend.

As Shelley's relationship with Jimmy proved to be more troublesome than it was worth, particularly with sporadic out-and-out physical abuse, she looked for a way out.

For whatever reason that no one will ever understand, Shelley tried to protect Jimmy's unruly character at all costs. It was a relationship made in hell and wasn't what Shelley had hoped for or wanted.

From time to time, Shelley had to wear sunglasses at work because of a black eye. It infuriated Noble to no end, as she kept telling Shelley to dump Jimmy.

Once when the girls were invited for a Sunday dinner at Shelley's parents' home, they had to lie about how she ran into the door to get the shiner.

Because Noble felt that no man should hit a woman, she was no fan of Jimmy and made it known all the time, in spite of Shelley's stance.

Jimmy just shrugged off her comments by telling her, "It was no one's business, so stay out of it."

Nonetheless, Shelley continued to defend Jimmy, and Noble told Shelley that if it happened again, she would report him to the police.

Even Jeffrey pulled Jimmy aside one day in the lunchroom and advised him that he better conduct himself properly; otherwise, he would do something about it.

Smugly Jimmy would shrug his shoulders and tell everyone to "Mind your own damn business. Shelley is my girl, and I will do as I damn well please!"

One time when Shelley came to work all banged up, Steve became so worried that he took his Jimmy's brother aside and said, "Bobby if you don't do something about this situation, Jimmy will be forbidden to work here or visit here again, and I will call the cops on him. Do you understand?"

Bobby pleaded with Steve to let him speak to Jimmy first. Sadly, Jimmy told Bobby the same thing as he told the others, "That it was nobody's business except his."

Regrettably, Bobby was torn between his love and protection for his brother and the safety of Shelley.

He knew that if he began to take steps to protect Shelley that all hell would break loose with his already troubled marriage, and he would no doubt lose his brother in the process.

Bobby tried to distance himself over this issue, particularly around his wife and Jimmy. He kept conversations light about the artists and places he'd traveled, and yet there were times when Evie looked right through him, without saying a word.

Evie knew that it was only a matter of time before everything blew up because Jimmy was out of control.

As the months passed by, Shelley became more and more depressed with Jimmy and told him that their relationship was over. She told him that she could no longer take the abuse, lying to everyone that they were in love and protecting him from this unbearable situation.

Jimmy smirked at Sheeley and said, "I don't believe it. You love me, and I love you. We are meant to be together."

Still, Shelley tried begging Jimmy to let her go and not call her or show up at her apartment at all hours of the day and night. She even asked Mrs. Alvarez to change the locks. But Jimmy couldn't get it through his head and continued to contact Shelley anyway he could.

The times he showed up unannounced, Noble threatened Jimmy that she would do something even if Shelley would not. It pissed Jimmy off, and he told Noble that he would kill her if she came between them.

Noble unafraid of Jimmy told him, "bugger off."

Noble then told Shelley and Jeffrey what he said to her and warned both of them of his cruel developing behavior.

When Bobby asked Jimmy what was going on, Jimmy would say, "Shelley and I are taking a break, and are seeing other people but that he was going to marry her."

Sometime after this, when Bobby came by the offices, Noble grabbed him as he was walking by the "bullpen" and read him the riot act about Jimmy's actions and what he said to Noble and others.

Bobby reluctantly said to Noble, "What do you want me to do, call the police on my brother?"

Noble responded by saying, "Hell, yes. If you don't, I will!"

Because of Bobby's busy schedule traveling, he sometimes did not see Jimmy for weeks on end, so it was no surprise when Jimmy wasn't there when the police came to Bobby's house after Shelley was murdered!

Though Evie and Bobby stayed in the house that they bought together, they were officially separated and had filed for divorce. Nonetheless, they decided that it would be cheaper for them at that moment to maintain a good relationship, since both were having affairs and were now using the house as a stop-over and to allow Jimmy to live there rent-free.

After the police informed them of their investigation, Evie started crying so much that Bobby wrapped his arms around her. Neither one of them could believe what they were hearing.

Bobby's heart was aching since he made it public only a few months prior that he and Shelley were together.

In Chicago at the merger meetings, Bobby took Shelley by the hands on the dance floor, in front of everyone and said to her aloud that he was in love with her.

As if planned, the band began to play "The Last Dance." Sammy Cahn and Jimmy Van Heusen wrote it.

Standing and holding Shelley, Bobby started to sing to her, "They're dimming the lights, the orchestra is yawning. We are alone on the floor. I want to hold you like this forever and more. Save your first dream for me tonight."

Everybody clapped their hands and cheered except one. Mysteriously, Jimmy's comment was,

"Congratulations, I hope you are both happy in your next lives." (Not life, but lives). Oddly, no one knew at that moment what this meant.

When the police asked where Jimmy might be, all that Evie and Bobby could say was, "They didn't know and why?"

The police told them that he was a person of interest since a neighbor across the street from where the Shelley's lived saw someone leaving the apartment who fit his description.

Neither Evie or Bobby could grasp what the police were saying. How could he, if it was Jimmy?

Of course, it could, Bobby thought. His jealousy was always very apparent. And yet...

Curiously, the evening that Shelley was killed, there was another girl murdered in kind of the same way, but in another part of town, south of Hollywood in Manhattan Beach. Neither precinct was aware of the other murder, until much later.

As a secretary, Charlotte Fleming was 23 years young with hazel eyes and blonde hair who worked at the aircraft company of William Williams in El Segundo, California.

All accounts last saw Charlotte at the Lighthouse Jazz Club in Hermosa Beach. According to witnesses and from the manager, she was with the drummer that night, leaving the club around 2:30 AM.

In the morning, her body was found in her apartment on Manhattan Ave by the manager when she went into the apartment to fix the air conditioner.

The coroner was able to determine that her death was early in the morning, and the police were now seeking anyone's knowledge or information about the long blonde-haired drummer who seemed to have disappeared.

By now, the police had obtained footage from the video camera tape in the security office of the apartment complex that placed the drummer as a possible suspect in the murder.

The Music Disc Murder
Chapter 8

The cops who were working on Shelley's murder found some new pieces of evidence. After taking the sheets and pillowcases to process in the crime lab to find anything that might be used to trace back to the suspected killer, they found a journal that was between the mattress and box spring that listed Shelley's friends, including the men in her life.

Each man would be investigated for sure. There was much about Rudy Stringer and the partying that took place in Laurel Canyon, which included some of the "hook-ups" that Shelley encountered while dating Rudy.

There was much about Jimmy and the beatings that she endured, and despite her love for him, initially, she didn't want to leave him. However, in the end, she had to leave him for her own sanity and health.

Included in the journal were many comments made by and from Noble and Jeffrey and Shelley's reasoning to stay with Jimmy. There was the whole incident with Richard's gifts and his affection for her, but she didn't want to be involved. Shelley did think that Richard was an alright person, as written in the notes, but he seemed to also shadow Jimmy as a "hot head" in his blow-ups and reactions.

Finally, there was an entry in the journal that night that included one word in it, "Richard"! The pen that she was using was stuck in between the pages. So, it looked like it was stashed under the mattress quickly and with purpose.

During the examination by the police, Bobby was instructed to go to the precinct for questioning, not only for his involvement but also about his brother Jimmy, who they could not locate. The cops had hoped that he could shed additional light on the case.

Bobby informed them that he and his wife were about to obtain a divorce so that he and Shelley could soon be married. Appeased somewhat by his supplementary information, the police turned their attention back to Jimmy. However, Bobby could not give them any more news about his whereabouts as Bobby had been out of town when the murder took place.

As Bobby left the station, he was beside himself regarding the path of the police investigation. He couldn't believe that his brother would have done such a horrible act.

Then the Lieutenant who was working on the case, alongside Murphy, told the Sergeant that he was not ready to rule out Richard and so stated it.

He stated, "After speaking with Steve Connelly, where Shelley worked, it seemed to me very peculiar that Richard would suddenly go to Cleveland or wherever since no one can locate him either. To me, we have two potential suspects in this murder. Who's to say that they mutually were not involved somehow?"

As part of his job, Lieutenant Long had to visit Mr. & Mrs. Wright's home to inform them of what happened and if they knew anything else that would help in the investigation. They did not.

Mrs. Wright was distraught beyond belief, living through something more than she ever wanted to experience. Her only daughter murdered. She said out loud, "What else could happen at this point?"

Mr. Wright asked several questions of Long, as much as Long asked Mr. Wright. Neither man had anything else that could help them in solving her death, and the Lieutenant told them that he would be in touch and left after a couple of hours.

As the Sergeant continued reading the additional entries in Shelley's journal, it mentioned a record retail location in the San Fernando Valley called, Sugar Shack Records. The manager's name Rudy Stringer was stated time and time again with hearts drawn next to his name. And unlike Jimmy and Richard, there was never a negative statement written about Rudy. So, "Who was this guy," thought Murphy?

After agreeing with the Lieutenant that Rudy needed to be questioned, the cops set upon the record store to question him, who, like the other persons of interest, seemed to be absent from his place of business.

Fortunately. after learning his whereabouts from the assistant manager, Blinky, he was found at his apartment, albeit a bit stoned from "pot," when he opened the door for the police.

Unconcerned about his condition, they did not arrest Rudy but asked him to accompany them to the station for questioning.

Sobering him up, they found out that though he and Shelley continued to be involved in a friendship basis only. Their original intimate relationship had ended quite a few months prior when she told him that she was going to marry Bobby.

Rudy then told Murphy, "After she broke up with Jimmy, Shelley and I were an item off and on for about a year. However, I was hounded by both Richard and Jimmy separately and were threatened to stop my affair with Shelley."

Rudy went on, "Richard had been drinking when he came there banging on the door at 10 AM on a Monday. He intimidated my salesclerk, who had just opened the store. Jimmy, on the other hand, waved a gun at one of the night clerks and was drunk as well."

Neither incident was ever reported to the police but was conveyed to Bobby regarding these two occurrences, since he was the sales rep for the store at the time.

Nothing like it ever happened again, so Rudy surmised that Bobby had taken care of the situation with the two guys.

Long and Murphy seemed to run into nothing but a dead-end, which of course, frustrated the hell out of them.

Normally there were telltale signs before or after the murder to assist them in locating the killer. Here there was none.

The police only found bits of pieces that did not include any substantial evidence to either Richard or Jimmy, let alone anyone else and yet!

Digging deeper, Murphy decided to look into George Hill's alibi and history, after hearing about the night of Jeffrey's party and the events that unfolded.

After obtaining information from the police database, Murphy found out that George was a transplant from the San Francisco Bay area, where he built a reputation of breaking up couples, primarily gay.

Jeffrey never knew George had a criminal record.

George battered some of his boyfriends and was quite the jealous type of anyone getting close to his lovers and ended up in jail several times. So, Murphy began an investigation on his life in LA to see if it correlated with any of the San Francisco Police Department (SFPD) reports.

According to the Sergeant, his findings of Mr. Hill and his relationship with Jeffrey, together with his reactions and actions to both Shelley's might link together the possible motive that George was the one involved with her murder.

The problem, of course, was that there was no evidence found that linked him to her death, except for his obsessiveness for Jeffrey.

When questioned at his home in Sherman Oaks, the police did not find any further reasons to pursue George, yet Murphy remained suspicious and decided to have a tail placed on him to be sure.

Murphy was determined to rule out every potential suspect in finding Shelley's killer.

The Music Disc Murder
Chapter 9

Leaving Charlotte's apartment, Jimmy was frantic as
to what had happened. They were both a little drunk
when they got back to her place and continued to fool
around dancing and singing and eventually fell
together into her bed. There they started to make
love, but something happened. Jimmy stripped out of
his clothes and jumped back on the bed when
Charlotte got panicky because Jimmy grabbed her
and aggressively tried to turn her over on her
stomach to strip her clothes off.

Not enjoying the roughness of Jimmy, Charlotte found
herself beginning to fight him as she didn't like what
was happening and told him to stop. Either he didn't
hear her and just ignored her, but he managed to rip
her panties off her, and as she continued to fight him,
she turned her face towards him, and somehow, her
neck broke.

Jimmy in his wild behavior to have sex with Charlotte
did not know immediately at the time, but after trying
to shift her body around, he gazed up from what he
was trying to do and looked at her and saw that she
was not moving with him and stared at her eyes and
immediately and forcibly jumped backward off of her.

Jimmy then stared at her for what seemed to be
several minutes and did not know what to do. Still a
bit drunk, he got himself dressed and went to the
bathroom to splash cold water on his face.

Looking in the mirror, Jimmy saw that same look he had seen before. The one of anger and then the "What the hell did I do" frightened face.

He knew he had to vanish, go someplace, get out of town, but where. Struggling to maintain some sanity, he wondered if he should call the police and explain what had happened?

Then realizing he would be investigated! He couldn't risk that because he already had a record.

They would handcuff him and put him in jail. The thought of jail almost made Jimmy throw up.

Gathering the rest of his stuff, he headed out to his car and decided to drive south to San Diego to catch his breath and figure out what to do next.

He kept thinking over and over, "Should I call my brother to let him know what had happened and where I was headed?" But then another thought hit him like a ton of bricks because he'd have to explain both deaths!

Along the highway, Jimmy found a rest stop around 5:30 AM, where he pulled into and slept as the rain fell continuously.

Back at the precinct sometime around 7 AM, Sergeant Murphy was chasing down his leads, while Lieutenant Long and another officer had just headed out to Richard's apartment to check out what they could find.

After obtaining a warrant for his arrest and a search warrant for his apartment, since Richard had left town in a hurry, the Lieutenant got the complex manager to open his apartment #2167.

At first glance, it seemed tidy and organized enough, and yet the Lieutenant was keenly aware that something didn't feel right and so he and the officer began emptying drawers and looking into the closets.

Richard had a two-bedroom apartment with one bath. He, too, had a journal with pencil sketches of what appeared to be a girl with long hair, big round eyes, and a smile. Very few words were used in describing the girl, but there must have been thirty or forty of them.

When the officer started to extract boxes from the guest room closet, he noticed that there were Polaroid pictures of the same girl in a variety of places.

"Lieutenant have a look at these," the officer said.

When the Lieutenant observed the pictures, he realized that what was in Richard's journal was Shelley.

All the photos in the box were her as if he was tracking her every move.

There were even dates and places written on the bottom of each picture to note when and where the picture had been taken.

Eerie, to say the least, Richard was obsessed with Shelley that caused the Lieutenant to substantiate that it was probably Richard who killed Shelley.

He had never seen such a detailed photographic history of anyone, even when he was with the FBI. They generally never had such a reason to track someone's every move in this way, though it had been used in excess once over a movie star and the President.

Long found it to be disturbing, to say the least, that caused the Lieutenant to want to know more about Shelley and who she was.

Looking through the box, Long found pictures of Shelley at night, dancing at clubs and sitting in restaurants.

Pictures were taken of her at her apartment and on weekends when she dated Jimmy, Rudy, and of course, recently with Bobby.

Had these gotten into the wrong hands, they could have been used to blackmail Shelley. It was scary stuff, and now Richard had vanished.

Long kept reflecting on what was in Richard's journal that he repeated over and over again, "Now is the time, it's now or never."

What did this mean? Only Richard could answer this, and he was nowhere to be found.

The Music Disc Murder
Chapter 10

When ElectroDisc took over the MAR label and distribution company, it was renamed Music Disc Distribution. There was much hubbub news in the industry about what would happen and who would be the President and what the two companies would look like after the merger.

The meetings took place in Chicago at the famed Princess Hotel. The Club part was famous for the risqué uniforms worn by the staff, both guys and girls.

Men and women wore black short shorts that were skintight, white shirts, with one button above their navel, that looked like they were drawn on their chests and breasts. The shirts included highlights of pink lapels and pink socks and black high heeled shoes for the girls. The men wore black laced up shoes that had extra heels that made a noise like tap shoes. It was a sight to be seen, truly a circus.

The English and their weird way of entertainment and business opted for this rather splashy and gaudy place. Some say that the Mob controlled it, but if so, it was never proven.

Right across from the Drake and the Oak Street Beach, the massive Princess stood, twenty-four stories high. It was built during the Roaring Twenties, when the Chicagoans both legit and non-legit benefitted from the large hotel, with its many rooms and ballrooms. Some rooms housed poker, while others housed blackjack and slot machines. Though you had to be part of the "in crowd" to be allowed into these rooms, it was never empty even in the daytime.

For Music Disc, preliminary meetings were held for two days while the management from each group worked out the details and press release information.

Meanwhile, the sales and promotions staffs were free to visit Chicago on their own, which allowed for some personal entertainment and relationships to evolve.

Shelley Noble was flown in separately, courtesy of Carlo. But she was registered as an assistant for his presentations to ElectroDisc and stayed with him during those five days.

Shelley Wright was also flown in to do the same but was afforded a room by herself, though Carlo did tell her that if anyone wanted to know where Noble was staying, it was with her.

The entire five days seemed to go well, except as noted:

1.   Richard, who was instructed to be part of the MAR transition team, appeared most of the time reckless, drunk, and obnoxious towards Shelley Wright in particular.

Unfortunately, when this was obvious to many of the staff, Noble was not around to help Shelley out, as she was with Carlo assisting him with his meetings.

In attendance, it was very apparent to all when, at an evening cocktail party, Richard walked up to Shelley and poured a drink down her blouse and laughed out loud about it.

Bobby and Evie, who attended the function without Jimmy at their side, came to Shelley's rescue, only this time, Bobby punched Richard straight in his face.

Richard staggered back and then raced towards Bobby screaming and cussing but was held back by some of the other MAR staff. They then walked Richard back to his room to sober up.

Jimmy had been absent during the fracas, but later found out about it and just laughed. He thought it funny that Richard was still trying to score with Shelley, after his own failed attempt. And other than giving his best wishes to the newly coined couple, he remained somewhat hidden during the Chicago meetings.

2.   Later that night, Shelley found herself alone in her room with Bobby, in which they decided to cement their affair. They also agreed to share this information aloud to all since they were in love and wanted everyone to know it.

3.   On the third day of the meetings, when the lights were dimmed, and the projector flashed the

first picture on the screen, it said, "Welcome to The Shotgun Wedding," from your Friends at ElectroDisc, LTD, London.

Fading into view was a picture of a shotgun and a bride.

Everyone was stunned at the cleverness of the new management, particularly as they started to roll out the new organization team.

Carlo was named the New Co-President, as was a new person, by the name of Evie Columbo.

It seemed that unbeknownst to most though Bobby knew, she had been in a serious relationship for some time, with Sir Taylor Douglas, the Owner, and CEO of ElectroDisc. As such, she was found to be the most qualified and was given the opportunity combined with Carlo of running this new division that would include film development.

Bobby, who was standing next to Shelley, was in shock. Shelley looked at him and said, "Did you know about this?"

"Hell no, but I did surmise that something was going on!" Bobby said, and then just shook his head, smiling.

It was beyond belief that his ex-wife would hold something like this from him. Yet, now he understood why there were many trips to Dallas, New York, and London that took place. She never let on that she was up for the job, only that she was in a relationship with Sir Douglas.

David, who was the Branch Manager, saw that his name was still listed as the Branch Manager. And though he expected to be let go in the merger, he figured that Carlo must have had something to say about it.

The rest of the morning went about as usual with artists from country to rock performing in between the presentations by the management teams and what was expected from each division.

Evie, who was with Sir Taylor backstage, finally came out from behind the screen to introduce herself, followed by Carlo.

Applause and cheers followed for the new team as Sir Douglas walked out behind them to show his support for both of them.

Almost everyone knew Carlo, but only a few people knew of Evie outside of the group at MAR's Sun Valley office.

While on stage, she never mentioned that she had been married to Bobby, which seemed odd at the time, but knowing that they were both in the final process of their divorce, it didn't bother Bobby. And he told Shelley so.

Despite MAR employees asking Richard to apologize to Shelley before the close of the meetings, he opted just to put it aside and forget about it.

After everyone flew back to their homes and offices, MAR offices were all abuzz with what happened in the Windy City.

Within two weeks, the teams from each label group and their responsibilities changed hands, and the home offices for the new Music Disc in New York, and LA began to ramp up.

Bobby and Evie went back to maintaining their household, separately, mainly for convenience, until Evie made the move to Sir Douglas's.

Traveling back and forth, neither Bobby or Evie saw each other for a week or so, leaving Jimmy by himself. After all, it was the record business.

With Evie and Carlo setting up their new offices in Century City, Shelley Noble made frequent trips to be with him in his new digs. And while Sun Valley made no real objections to this, Carlo made sure that it was approved, and travel was paid for her driving there and back.

David continued his role as did Steve, but now Steve was getting antsy to do something else and started to look around outside the music and record business. He had spent his time as one of the oldest employees who started with ComAmerica and felt that he moved down the corporate ladder, rather than up.

The Music Disc Murder
Chapter 11

As Murphy continued his investigation, he analyzed the on and off love affair between Rudy and Shelley. It had materialized after Jimmy, or was it because of Jimmy, seemed to be more of the answer.

Shelley met lots of celebrities because of Rudy's house in Laurel Canyon and his store in the San Fernando Valley. It was where artists and managers alike frequented, without being bothered.

Located in Sherman Oaks, on Ventura Blvd., it was referred to as the "Mini Tower Records," with a little of Virgin Records thrown in for its appearance.

Besides all of the U.S. album releases, Rudy stocked much of the U.K., German and French releases, since the Beatles, Stones and other bands coming out of Europe were so hot.

Rudy also prided himself on the fact that if Warner's released something here in the States, then he would locate it throughout Europe and purchase the import version as well.

The store held regular acoustic performances by many of the famous bands along with the local bands trying to make it. They were always free, but you had to have a ticket to get into the weekend nights event.

The tickets were given to those that purchased albums from the bands appearing, and when the store reached its capacity, Rudy would issue a rain check ticket any other event.

Shelley was always in awe of the people walking into the store just to shop. It was the Valley's hottest place to be.

As an almost older hippie who had co-written a few songs with some now-famous bands, and living off the residuals, Rudy was fortunate enough to purchase a house and lived next door to a very famous rock and roll star in Laurel Canyon off Kirkwood.

There he was almost constantly partying either at his own house or some other star-studded home.

On any day on what was called "Lookout Mountain," you might see, Joni Mitchell, The Phillips, band members from The Byrds or CS&N, Peter Tork and a host of others.

Down at the end of the street was a small convenience store called "Canyon Country Store," where everyone bought their goods. In a way, it was a little community within itself that belonged in Northern California like Mill Valley or some other hippie place.

If you didn't watch where you were going, on the Canyon drive, you could find yourself lost in the hills that overlooked LA, on bright sunny days or star scattered nights.

Shelley was introduced to them all, as Rudy made his rounds nightly. Never-ending drugs and booze flowed, and on nights of passion, one might be hooked up with anyone as substance exploitations took place.

One night, Jimmy, through a fluke, accidentally encountered Rudy and Shelley at a party and ended up having sex with Shelley when Rudy was passed out, and Shelley was stoned from a mushroom concoction.

Though Shelley could not recall what happened with the encounter, Jimmy made mention of it several days later while at the Sun Valley offices, which disturbed Shelley that it even took place.

Shelley was so upset by this possible encounter with Jimmy that she pressed Rudy about that night, and he told her, "I can't remember."

Rudy went on to say that "Shelley, you need to let it go if you don't remember it either. It's not that important!"

But Shelley was distraught that she would have allowed herself to be that vulnerable, and so this was the beginning of the end with her relationship with Rudy.

She never again wanted to be taken for granted or advantage of and stopped attending parties on "The Canyon."

Noble attempting to be her big sister, had warned Wright time and again that she better be careful.

But Wright would smile and say, "I have everything and everybody under control." Though in the end, she did not.

When the affair ended with Rudy, it was because of too many parties and too many drugs, yet they remained friends.

After Jimmy found out, he thought it was his time to shine again, but little did he know that Shelley was laying low and not looking for love or another man.

It was her time to work and continue at The Actors Workshop, yet, this is not what happened.

Returning to UCLA to continue her lessons, Shelley met an older Professor that would teach her the fine art of speaking in front of the camera or on stage.

Almost immediately, he took a liking to her as he thought that her looks would become famous even within Hollywood, with its many beautiful wannabees.

The professor worked after class in the evenings with Shelley on her phrasing.

When she left each evening, he felt that his feelings were always on the verge of affection and possible intimacy. Yet the professor held back, not knowing how Shelley would have reacted if he had made an advance. So, he kept it to himself.

Hence, he cared for her from afar, and that was that.

Shelley never knew his feelings but sensed that he really liked her, and so it went no further than teacher and pupil.

Ironically, the professor had just introduced her to one of his prior star pupils, who had become the newest up and comer sci-fi directors.

The former pupil liked Shelley's voice as well as her looks. So, the director had arranged a screen test for a movie he was working on filming. He had her scheduled unbeknownst to most except for Noble, for the week following her death. (His movie went on to be one of the biggest hits in the '70s).

The Music Disc Murder
Chapter 12

The first time that Bobby spent any time with Shelley
was when Evie was in London for a couple of weeks.

Bobby was showcasing a famous band from Germany
at the Whiskey, and most of the girls from the office
went there that night as part of the "all-girls night"
for Jill's birthday bash.

Bobby was representing the label along with the
promotion guy Billy Vee.

Billy was responsible for dragging the local rock radio
stations to be part of the festivities for the evening.

On stage, it was the job of the DJ's from the stations
to introduce each member of the band, which drove
the crowd into a frenzy.

The national music and political magazines covered
the event, and there was a boatload of industry
people hanging out as usual, for the free libations and
food.

Shelley had recently broken up with Rudy and was
trying to go at it alone, wanting some time to
replenish herself, particularly after Jimmy and Rudy.

Noble, Shelley, and the office girls were there to hang
out and get crazy that night, which is exactly what
happened.

During the evening, Noble and Wright became extremely loose and ended up dancing on the floor together, where the crowd had opened up space for the two women to party as the band sang their butts off.

When the song was over, even the band applauded for the girls' performance.

Spent, and a bit tipsy, Noble and Wright started looking for a ride home as the bar closed.

Bobby was finishing paying the club when he came walking by and asked them if they had a ride?

Nobel told Bobby, "It would be our pleasure if you would take us home, we wouldn't be able to make it on our own."

Bobby laughed and said, "No problem, just give me a minute to wrap up everything here."

Since Bobby was technically the label rep and in charge of the night, he hadn't drunk anything but club soda. It was his job to keep the new act safe and didn't want any bad first impressions.

After locating his car, he drove back to the entrance and blew the horn.

Noble being the comedian, said to Shelley, "Our carriage has arrived Madame Boleyn."

To which, Shelley replied, "I hope I don't lose my head or my heart then?"

Both girls laughed as they walked outside and into Bobby's car.

It was a classic 1962 Buick Skylark with bench seats, so all three were squeezed in the front.

Bobby could feel the heat radiating from Shelley's leg against his, as he turned corners.

It was a bit unnerving as he kept looking at her quickly to see if she was doing it on purpose or not.

Without even a nudge or glance back, Bobby thought that he was imagining that it was happening.

With Noble against the door, the three of them were cozy and very close.

Bobby's other senses were working overtime as he could smell Shelley's perfume that was probably infused by her perspiration after dancing for a couple of hours.

The girls were initially chatty talking about the band and how good looking they were, when Bobby said, "Gee, you do know I am here, what am I chopped liver?"

The girls laughed at him, and Shelley said, "Bobby, sure you're good looking but married, so we have to discount you since you aren't on the market!"

Noble laughed again and replied, "Yep, but if you were..."

Then Noble cast a big smile his way, and the girls laughed again.

When he finally got them home, they had fallen asleep with Noble's head against the window of the car and Shelley's head resting on Bobby's right arm and shoulder.

After he gently woke them up and they said their goodnight, Shelley leaned over to Bobby, smiled at him and looked into his eyes, and said, "Thank You very much for bringing us home safely and for being the gentleman you are."

Then as she turned to leave the car, she turned back around towards Bobby, who was looking at her leave, and she kissed him on the lips that seemed like five minutes long. Then quickly, she stepped out of the car and waved at Bobby as he sat there a bit stunned.

The girls looked at Bobby sitting in the car the turned and then scampered in through their front door.

Bobby realized then that he was still not moving and placed the car in drive and drove out of the roundabout smiling at himself.

To Bobby, it was a night to remember.

Inside the apartment, Noble was scolding Shelley for being so brazen.

But Shelley laughed and said out loud, "But it was good!" as she closed her bedroom door.

The Music Disc Murder
Chapter 13

Spending so much time in London, Evie felt some resentment towards Bobby but knew that it would not be fair that he now loved Shelley, especially since her own life had turned around. Yet, in a way, she reflected on an earlier time when life was carefree and not made by money or position.

Staring out the window at the Thames, the offices of ElectroDisc were just off the Blackfriars Pier. Evie compared them constructively with any American corporation office, as she looked up and down the river...

Almost all the younger "kids" in the office dressed in "MOD" fashion, while the accountants and barristers usually dressed in a suit with a vest. After all, it was England, and proper attire was always the best option and standard for business attire, even more than its cousins in America.

Sir Douglas certainly achieved much in his forty-five years, going from the son of a chimney sweeper to the private owner of a very large corporation. Never married but fathered two children, ages 11 and 13, he made sure that they were well-taken care of, along with their mothers.

Private schools and limousines to chauffeur them back and forth, the children lived in luxury beyond anything that Evie ever knew.

It was so different than her upbringing, being raised in Leavenworth, Kansas, within the upper-lower class folk.

The town was known for its prison mostly.

Her parents had a very small farm that barely supported the three of them. They lived down the road from her Mother's parents. The grandparents, cared for Evie since her Mom had to take a job in town to help out with expenses, while her Dad worked the fields.

And yet, here Evie was today in London, living an extravagant life with a new man who apparently would make her the happiest woman in the years to come. Life had changed for sure.

From almost the beginning, somehow, Evie and Taylor hit it off, both from a business sense as well as personally.

Taylor was very proper in his approach with Evie, as their closeness became real. He didn't want to compromise her life or come between her and Bobby.

Evie, in her Middle America politeness, explained to him that the relationship had ended a long time ago and that Bobby had moved on, and so she gave Taylor the green light to pursue her.

Nevertheless, Taylor wanted to make sure that everything was up and up between them and even asked, "Is there anything that I need to do regarding Bobby or Shelley?"

Evie responded by saying, "Nothing would be gained or required because they all were adults and living as they wanted to."

During the months that followed, Evie was introduced to his children as well as to his Manor, located in Saint Albans. There, a small herd of cattle, sheep, and horses were tended to.

Sprawling lands existed in St. Albans, which included his neighbor's farm, The Macintosh's,

Down the road, "The Macs" cared for chickens, pigs, and more sheep.

The Taylor children loved to visit since they didn't need to do anything like chores when they were at home. They just got to play with the other children, from St. Albans.

The house of Douglas, coat of arms included three white stars against the shield on a background of blue with the bottom of a red heart on white. The origin came from Sweden and France but was an ancient clan from the lowlands of Scotland.

Caring for the house and grounds were several maids and two butlers, that looked after the estate, with the hired groundskeepers.

There were five bedrooms and just as many bathrooms, with two sitting rooms in the seven thousand square foot Manor.

End to end with the stable, the farmhouse, swimming pool, and tennis court. There was also a guest house, which is where Evie initially stayed.

When the relationship became serious, she then moved into the Manor but stayed in another bedroom, so the children would not suspect anything.

When Taylor told her that he was going to bring her aboard and promote her to Co-President, she argued that it would look like nepotism, which he told her bluntly that he didn't care.

When she was introduced to his management group, the greying long-haired CEO, looked more like a 70's hippie than an executive of a multi-million-dollar company.

Before long, Evie was accepted as the American arm of the company and as "Sir Douglas's Girlfriend."

The Music Disc Murder
Chapter 14

As the days turned into weeks and then to months, Bobby began spending more time in the company of Shelley.

It Occurred first by accident. The Music Disc company had more events for its artists at stores like Tower Records or Rudy's place: Sugar Shack Records. Here the two Shelley's would attend along with other company personnel where Bobby was in charge to make sure that everything went smoothly.

Sometimes after these events, some of the company staff would go to another club and hang out for hours. Then they would finally get home in the wee hours of the morning, just in time to nap and go back to the office.

Once when Bobby took the girls home, after seeing Steely Dan, they invited Bobby in for a nightcap. Though a bit unsure, Bobby accepted and ended up falling asleep on the couch.

It was innocent enough. However, Evie thought otherwise, when Bobby came in the following morning to change his clothes.

Then when he tried to explain, she blow up for not calling, even though she had spent most of the night with Sir Taylor. Bobby was unaware of the tryst for the longest time.

It wasn't until months later when Evie informed Bobby that she wanted to separate since she was spending more and more time in London and New York. She went on to confess that she and Sir Taylor were an item and in love.

Bobby hadn't wanted to have children, and Sir Taylor was captivated enough with Evie that he agreed to have a child with her, providing they got married.

Evie had fallen for the well-established Englishman and told Bobby so and that she was sorry for keeping it a secret for so long.

On his side, Bobby was falling in love with Shelley, but she didn't know. She was so wrapped up spending more time at The Workshop along with trying out for a bit part at MGM for an up and coming sci-fi movie.

After Rudy, Shelley decided that she needed to stay focused on her life and not look for love since she had had two different extremes of it. And though each one provided something in her life, it certainly wasn't what she was looking for.

When the news broke about Evie and Sir Taylor, the Music Disc company just shrugged their shoulders, since this was after all the record business and relationships and marriages were in a way a dime a dozen. Unfortunately, this also included the divorces that followed.

Jimmy, who was living at the house with Evie and Bobby, had some sympathy for Bobby and sanctimoniously told him that "there was plenty of fish..."

Yet Bobby wasn't interested in the many, only one, Shelley Wright.

One afternoon at the company/industry baseball game, Shelley was playing second base as Bobby rounded the first base and headed for second.

As the throw from the right-field came lobbing in, Shelley was able to scoop it off the dirt and collided with Bobby for the out.

"To bad for Bobby," she thought and turned to see that he was bleeding on his cheek where she had accidentally smacked him with the glove.

A bit stunned by the collision, Bobby was looking up at Shelley when she knelt and asked him, "Are you alright?"

Several team members rushed out of the dugouts to where Shelley and Bobby were when Richard stood over them, both edging out the other players and said, "He looks alright, though I would have killed him had it been me..."

The rest of the team looked at Richard and gave him crap for being so cold-hearted regarding the accident.

Jimmy, who had been playing third base, came over and said out loud, "What a bitch!" as he looked at Shelley. "How'd you like it if someone did that to you?"

Shelley, in a moment of absentmindedness, replied, "They have, and it will never happen again!" as she looked back at Jimmy with her steel-blue eyes.

The crowd knew what she meant, and Jimmy turned quickly and walked away from the crowd.

Richard, in his normal pity stance, just laughed at them and replied, "One day you all will get yours" and then marched off the field.

Looking back at Bobby in that moment and without saying anything, Shelley's heart skipped a beat and saw in his eyes the look that she had been waiting for. That look of true love.

Then a couple of teammates proceeded to help Bobby to his feet and walked him back to the dugout.

He was still gazing in Shelley's eyes as he sat down to recoup from the tumble.

In Shelley's mind, it was replaying every moment from the collision until his departure on the field.

She couldn't believe what she was thinking.

Did he feel the same thing that she just felt? "He must know," she said to herself. "It was so very apparent, wasn't it?"

When the inning was over, no one said anything to her except, "Are you okay?" "Boy, that was some hit."

No one said anything about Bobby, so was she dreaming, or was it real?

When the game was done, Shelley found Bobby putting his gear into his car and asked him, "How are you feeling?"

"Sore," he said, "Luckily, I got patched up with some ice, aspirin, and Neosporin. So, I am coming around slowly. Boy, can you pack a wallop!"

"I am so sorry, Bobby," Shelley said as she handed him his bat.

"I didn't think that anything like that would happen. But I guess the leather on the glove cut your face, and again, I am sorry."

"No problem Shelley. I've gotten hit like that before", though he couldn't remember when.

Bobby smiled at Shelley, and she at him, and he blurted out, "Do you want to grab a bite?"

As Shelley hesitated, she said, "Okay, as long as it is someplace easy and casual. I will have to find Noble and let her know."

Bobby said, "Sure, just tell her that I will bring you home, and it won't be late since I am tired too."

After finding Noble chit-chatting with Richard of all people, Noble told Shelley to have a good time.

She continued, "Not to be too late. We are supposed to get up early in the morning and go to Tower Sunset for an artist autograph signing."

Richard looked at Shelley and said to her, "Yah, we wouldn't want anything to happen to you or cause you any harm!"

Shelley looked at Noble and then back to Richard and said, "What do you mean?"

Richard replied, "Oh nothing, just that you have to be careful these days with the guys that are out there."

Shelley looked at Richard straight in the eyes and responded by saying, "I don't think I have to worry about Bobby like I've had to worry about you and my ex. Both of you guys are always looking for trouble, while Bobby is a gentleman."

Richard smirked and said, "You never know."

And with that, Shelley left to find Bobby.

Standing by his car with a puffy face, Shelley walked up to Bobby and said, "Okay, let's go."

After sliding into his classic Buick, Bobby drove over to the "Bob's Big Boy" casual restaurant in Burbank, on Riverside Drive. It was the closest and most casual of restaurants nearby and was inexpensive to boot.

Home of the original Double Deck Hamburger, it was a diner/coffee shop that served food twenty-four hours a day, seven days a week, and 365 days a year.

The studios that were close by kept it busy, and the restaurant competed with the commissaries on the movie lots during the day but owned the grip men and actors alike every night.

Shelley was feeling giddy in this impromptu date with Bobby. This was the first time that they both sat down together and alone without any of their associates or friends around them.

They opted to split a salad and "Pappy Parker's Fried Chicken and Waffles," and they took their time talking to each other about their lives, their current situations, and their dreams, which seemed to intermingle with each other's.

The late afternoon turned into a later night than expected as the two flirted with each other in their conversations. They seemed to be traveling on the same path and were, in a way, playing chess in their game of love.

Finally, Shelley said, "Oh my, it's late, I've got to get home. I am sorry."

Bobby replied, "No problem, I am bushed and need some rest after the fun day."

At this point, he reached out and patted her hand that was on the table.

Shelley smiled and said, "Yeah," and stood up as Bobby paid the check.

Driving Shelley back to her place, they continued some small talk, but Bobby didn't press anything since he didn't want to scare her off now that he had told her his situation with Evie. Nor did he want to come on strong, since he was feeling rather taken by her.

When they finally arrived back at her apartment, Shelley, who sat closer to the passenger window almost the entire way from the restaurant, reached over in what appeared to be a handshake gesture. But instead, as Bobby reached out his hand, she used his hand and arm to move face to face, looking into his eyes and softly kissed Bobby on the lips.

Bobby's heart seemed to skip a beat, and he returned the kiss in just the same manner, softly, with lips parting lightly. They continued touching each other's tongue, kissing each other gently over and over until all of a sudden, there was a knock on the passenger window.

It was Noble looking sternly at both of them, like a mother hen.

All three of them started laughing, and Shelley turned back to Bobby and said, "Goodnight. This was fun, and we need to do it again soon."

Bobby responded, "Absolutely, I agree. See you soon."

Shelley bounded out of the door, and the two girls went into the apartment, leaving Bobby smiling to himself as he drove away.

It was hours later that the girls finally went to sleep.

Noble kept prying everything out of Shelley about her and Bobby's evening and what she thought of him, and what was the situation with Evie?

Bobby replayed the night over in his mind as the car seemed to find itself back to his house all by itself.

Bits and pieces of Shelley's face flashed in front of his brain, her smile, her lips repeating something she had said, and her accent on certain words. His mind raced forward and backward to the past and to a future that included her in his life. It was all too surreal and frightening. "Did she feel it too," he thought, "or was it just his own desire and fantasy that was playing tricks on his thoughts?"

It was almost midnight, and the lights in his house were on in most of the rooms, which seemed a bit odd.

Getting out of his car, he walked up to the door where he heard music blaring, and he entered to find Jimmy half-naked with a girl in the same manner but tied up on a chair in the living room.

Her face was bruised and bloody, and she looked scared to death as Jimmy appeared to be in a trance weaving in front of her, without knowing that Bobby had come home.

Gone was the delight and joy of the night. Instead, fear and outrage of what was going on replaced Bobby's thoughts.

Bobby quickly shut off the music, which turned Jimmy towards him to see what had happened. His strange distorted face changed into this child's look of "I wasn't doing anything bad." But Jimmy knew that he was in trouble.

Bobby grabbed the throw blanket that was on the couch as he walked up to the poor girl and began untying her as Jimmy just stood there without moving.

Bobby then helped the girl to her feet, covered her up, and walked her to the dining room where he placed her on a chair. She was in shock, not saying a word as Bobby ran to the kitchen for some ice and a clean towel. After running some tepid water on the towel, he returned to the dining room and began to clean the girl's face.

When he was done, he told the girl to place the ice that was inside another towel over the left side of her face.

He then said, "Where are your clothes?"

The girl pointed towards Jimmy's room, and Bobby ran to the room to fetch them.

When he returned, Jimmy was standing near the girl and asked Bobby, "What are you going to do?"

Bobby replied, "I am cleaning her up to take her to the emergency. I want to make sure that she is Okay. And you need to figure out what you are going to do because the hospital will surely report this to the police."

Jimmy, in his smart-ass style, then said, "I don't care. We were having fun, and so if she got a little banged up? It's nobodies' business, but ours."

Bobby couldn't believe what he was hearing. His brother had become this ruthless and uncaring person that beat up women. He didn't care, but it could send him to jail for life.

In responding to Jimmy, he said, "Listen, you have a problem, and this girl, whoever she is," as he looked her way, "will undoubtedly report you to the police. I know I would, so you better think of something to do to amend this situation. Do you understand?"

Jimmy just shrugged his shoulders, grinned, and walked out of the room. Once again, he showed his true colors to Bobby that he didn't care.

By the time Bobby had gotten Jayne to the hospital, he had found out her name, occupation, and address.

She was a waitress at the Baked Potato, the jazz club on Lankershim and Ventura Blvds. She had been there for four years and was currently a law student at Cal State Northridge, finishing her last year there.

Tall, almost 6 feet, dirty blond hair and brown eyes she didn't seem to be the type for Jimmy, but apparently, he roped her into some promise otherwise Bobby couldn't believe that she would have gone along with his brother's shenanigans.

Bobby stayed with Jayne as the doctor and nurses set to fix her up. In the report, she stated that I had found her outside of the club where someone had roughed her up. Later Bobby told her that she had all the right in the world to report Jimmy, but she insisted that since Bobby had rescued her, she felt obliged to keep it under the radar. However, she would make sure that she would never do that again with anyone else.

The Music Disc Murder
Chapter 15

When the phone call came at 1:45 AM at Bobby and Evie's house three days after the murder, Bobby had recently returned from Vegas, after seeing several accounts, woke up in confusion. He wasn't exactly sure where he was. After all, his life had taken such a turn of events that he was not able to comprehend anything at the moment.

It was only last week that he and Shelley were making plans when they dined at El Coyote, their favorite Mexican Restaurant. They spent the better part of the evening discussing what would happen once Evie moved to New York, where Jimmy might live and where and when she and Bobby would move in together. Life was great; they both thought.

They had even made plans for the official meetings of each set of parents. They were on their way to being a couple. But then...

He had been in Phoenix at Zia Records for the "Kickin Boots" album release party. Then after waking up late the following morning, he decided to drive up route 93, which would take about 6 hours.

Bobby needed to be by himself and listen to some music and the air rushing by with all the windows open.

He and Evie had finalized their divorce and now had to decide on what to do with the house, since Jimmy was still technically living there, but who had disappeared. Even so, he thought, "I'll find an inexpensive apartment someplace or maybe shack up with another musician or company member until he figured things out, especially now with Shelley gone."

When they tracked down Bobby in Vegas at his hotel to tell him what had happened, he was in total shock.

He could not even begin to understand and got into his car and drove home in a trance. He just drove and drove thinking about Shelley. What would he do now?

The call jarred Bobby into reality, as Jimmy's voice came across with a staticky sound. He said, "Bobby, I am in jail in Tijuana, can you come and bail me out?"

Bobby, now totally awake, said, "Okay, but where in Tijuana, are you, and what did you do?"

Jimmy replied, "I'll tell you when you get here. It's gonna cost 5000 dollars, not pesos. Hurry, if you can, I am in real danger here." Then the phone went silent.

"Christ," thought Bobby, "He never told me where he was."

Jumping up, Bobby ran to his closest. In a shoebox tucked under some socks, he found an envelope, which included four one-thousand-dollar bills.

"Not enough," he thought. "Maybe Evie has some in her room. I will have to borrow it if she does".

Looking through Evie's drawers and things, he finally was able to scrape together a little over the $5000.

He dashed to the shower, and after getting dressed, he jumped into his car and began to drive to the border.

Bobby reckoned that it would take him about four or five hours to drive since it was now almost 3 AM, and he would certainly run into a little traffic in San Diego. Little did he know that it would take a bit longer than the typical day.

By the time Bobbie approached the "Baja border crossing," it was almost 9 AM.

Traffic was heavier than normal due to the highway construction of expanding the road from Mexico.

Bobby thought, "Wow, it's been a long time since I was down this far in San Diego. Everything changes".

After driving up to the border guard, it took almost an hour for Bobby to get into Tijuana, where he was quizzed over and over why was he visiting Mexico. Instead of telling the guards about his brother, Bobby decided on the idea of just telling them that he was on holiday. After sitting in his car for almost an entire hour, the guards finally let him pass through.

Frustrated by the lack of cooperation, because he didn't do anything, he finally found the Centro Policia.

Perhaps it was his attitude, after the incompetence at the border, but walking into the station, he felt that it was almost like walking into any American station, and unfortunately, it was noticed.

The station looked the same with a Sergeant on duty sitting high on a ramp above anyone standing on the floor.

The policeman finally looked up from his papers after Bobby stood there for five minutes and asked, "Si, ¿Cómo Puedo ayudarle."

Bobby immediately said, "Pardon me, but I do not speak Spanish."

"Oh, Okay," the Sergeant replied, "What can I do for you?"

Bobby explained who he was and why he was there, and after a few minutes of looking through the papers on his desk, the Sergeant turned to another officer and asked him some questions.

Bobby could only surmise where Jimmy might be held.

The Sergeant then turned back around and said to Bobby, "I am sorry, Señor, no one knows where your brother Jimmy might be." Perhaps if you knew where he called from, then we could locate him for you. Otherwise, I don't know what to tell you."

Bobby was beside himself. He was getting what seemed to be the runaround, and he didn't know what to do or where to go to find his brother. He didn't even know why he was down in Baja in the first place.

What happened to Jimmy, and why was he in jail, kept playing in his mind. "What the hell happened?"

Pacing in the station, Bobby decided that instead of arguing with the Sergeant to the point of himself possibly being thrown into jail, he opted to see if there was an Embassy located in Tijuana. Maybe they could help locate Jimmy.

Bobby asked the Sergeant if he knew where the U.S. Embassy was, and he grinned at Bobby and said, "Senor, I cannot be sure since I have never been there."

Bobby knew it was no use, so he walked out and got into his car and started driving around the main streets in hopes of locating it.

Fortunately, he found the consulate after driving up and down the streets, stopping anyone he found and asking over and over if anyone knew where it was.

The consulate, a young boy told him, was located at Ave. Tapachula # 96, Colonia Hipodromo, Tijuana, Baja California, Mexico.

Finally, locating it, he pulled his car into a parking spot and walked up to the American military personnel standing at the gates.

After explaining the situation to the soldiers, he was permitted to go in to discuss the matters with the consulate secretary.

Pleasantries exchanged when he met a helpful team of attaches and secretaries, but after several hours of phone calls and discussions, there was no additional information about the whereabouts of Jimmy.

The only thing that came out of the meetings and talks was that they would continue to search out his brother's whereabouts and that they would inform Bobby if they were able to find out anything.

Dejected, Bobby knew there was little that he could do except wait and spend the night or two and visit the consulate again in the morning to see if they were able to find out anything more.

However, when the day turned out to be just another runaround, he asked the consulate secretary if he should leave or stay.

Her response was, "I'd give it one more day to be on the safe side. Then if we are still looking and haven't located him, by all means, return home. We would contact you anyway once we found out anything. "

Bobby agreed and drove out to the beach to relax. He decided that in the morning, if there were still no news, he would return to Los Angeles.

That morning, the consulate had found out some news about Jimmy but was unclear where he was being held. They only told Bobby that they had connected with someone that had seen him, and they were trying to find out his location.

Tired, hungry, and mad that his brother never told him where he was being held, Bobby decided to drive back to L.A. For the moment, Bobby felt lost and could not even figure out what his next move would be.

His life had fallen apart. First, his girlfriend is killed, and then his brother goes missing! Was there a connection?

The Music Disc Murder
Chapter 16

Little to go on, Lieutenant Long kept digging around
Richard's involvement with Shelley. Did they ever
date or go out? Were they ever intimate? By
interviewing the office staff, a trickle of information
began to unravel that hadn't been observed before.

Richard was, as it turned out, the main person that
Shelley went to for all kinds of problems or questions
on how to do her job when she was first hired. As
such, Richard was all too willing to assist her, and
through this, he felt that she liked him very much.

However, as it was, Shelley got involved with Jimmy
and then with Rudy and eventually with Bobby that
almost destroyed Richard. Regrettably, he was
obsessed with her and started his unsolicited gifts.

Being able to ascertain a new position that paid more
money than he ever earned within the company,
Richard felt and believed that he would be able to
woo Shelley to his side and to love him.

Unfortunately, right before he could accomplish this,
she told Steve about Richard and his gift-giving, that
denied him from ever getting his chance.

Furthermore, Richard knew that his position and the
move to the Hollywood office would only push his
face out of view and out of the picture. So despite a
better situation, his chances were probably over.

Distraught over this dilemma, Richard planned another tactic. He thought for once and for all, it would give him a chance at proving his feelings for Shelley. Still, when his own party failed, it threw Richard into a spiral that he could no longer contain.

When the Camaro that Richard was driving pulled into his Uncle's driveway on Starkweather Ave in Lincoln Park, it was nearly midnight. Not wanting to wake him up, Richard fell asleep in his car but was woken around 8 AM.

Uncle Dom, short for Dominik, also spelled Dominic, so frightened Richard that he rammed the opened door on Dom.

Richard apologized as he untangled himself and stepped out of the car and hugged his Uncle. In disbelief that he was home, Dom kept squeezing Richard.

After a few minutes, they both went into the house.

Dom told Richard to sit down on the blue and white couch that was still covered in plastic. His wife, Hanna, installed the cover when it was new, almost 15 years ago, and before she passed away.

Dom couldn't bear to change anything in the house, and so it remained the same as when she was alive.

When Dom returned from the kitchen with the two coffees in his hands, he sat across from Richard and handed him the cup and said, "Ok, my boy, there has to be a reason why you have driven home this time. What is it?"

Richard relayed the status of his new job, promotion, and general things about his life, yet he held back the most important part.

Looking deep into Richard's eyes, Dom said, "it's all about a girl, right?"

Nodding his head a few times, Richard said, "yes, but a terrible thing has happened, and I do not know what to do?"

"What could be so bad," Dom started to say when, Richard reacted and blurted out, "I may have killed my chance, I may have killed Shelley."

Dom was stunned by what his nephew said. He then told Richard to try and remain calm, get some rest, and they would discuss all the details later.

It wasn't till the following morning that Richard woke up, sleeping in his old teenage bed upstairs. The bed faced the window looking out at the old elm tree, where Richard climbed up and down as a young boy. In waking up, all he could remember was Shelley's naked body lying there and not moving.

When Richard came downstairs, he sat across from Dom in the kitchen and began to repeat the entire story.

Through his label connections, Richard obtained tickets and backstage passes to go to the Pilgrimage Theatre on Cahuenga to be part of the Don Ellis Concert. Because he knew that Shelley was a fan, he invited her to attend the concert with him. However, she thought that other office members were attending it as well but later found out that it was just Richard and her.

Deciding it was alright, Richard picked up Shelley at her apartment, even though she was a bit confused with the evening. However, in the car, Richard offered Shelley some pot, and after smoking it, she became more relaxed, and by the time they got to the theater, both were high and laughing at most of what they talked about.

The concert was great, at least as much as they could remember, meeting the band members and hanging out after the show.

Driving back to her apartment, Shelley was feeling amorous from the drinks and pot by the time they got back to her place.

There she invited Richard in, running into her bedroom and told Richard to have a seat.

Noble wasn't home that night as she went to Vegas with Jeffrey to see one of the Music Disc bands perform at the MGM Hotel.

What seemed to be a very short flash of time, Richard found Shelley standing in front of him with only a short filmy see-through robe.

Standing up and without saying a word, he picked her up and walked back to her room, where he gently placed her down on the bed.

Stunned and happy at the same time, he began ripping off his clothes.

Richard could barely contain himself, knowing that all his dreams were coming true.

But the rage that was still inside him after all this time, waiting for her, took over, and he shoved himself inside of her and began heaving back and forth until they both passed out.

When he awoke, he found that she must have bled on the bed, next to her face that seemed to have come out of her nose.

Upon further examination of Shelley, it freaked Richard out since there was blood also between her legs. He looked at his stomach and private parts and noticed the dried blood. She looked dead, and she was not breathing, he thought. She didn't move.

Scared beyond anything he ever experienced, he got up off the bed abruptly. Suddenly, he felt guilty and sick at the same time, believing that he killed her.

Richard asked himself, "What the hell did I do?" He didn't want to touch her for fear that her body would be cold. She looked unresponsive in the moonlight that shone through her open, draped window.

Without checking if he touched anything else in her room, he quickly put his clothes on and left the apartment. It was early in the morning, as he could remember, sometime after 3 AM.

His private parts ached as he sat down in his car. He didn't know what the hell happened. He just wanted to get out of there.

Unaware to Richard, as he peeled out of the courtyard, the lights from his car woke up Jimmy, who was asleep in his car across the street.

Walking across the street in the moonlight, Jimmy opened the door to Shelley's apartment, where it was spooky silent.

Having stolen Bobby's keys when he was out of town, Bobby made a copy of the key for Shelley's apartment and Bobby's safety deposit box.

Jimmy had kept track of Shelley unsuspected by anyone else. It was his way of loving her from afar, at least that is what he told himself.

Pausing in the doorway, Jimmy stood for a moment while the neighbor across the street who was out walking her dog, saw a light come on. There, with his back towards the street, the neighbor could see only long blonde hair on a man who then closed the door behind him.

Jimmy calmly walked into the living room, then stopped in the dead silence.

As he crept closer to Shelley's room, a wave of anticipation over-took him, and he jumped back after pushing the door open.

There, looking at Shelley's naked body lying on the bed, he saw blood on the sheets. He was horror-struck by the sight.

Feeling lightheaded, he grabbed hold of the door frame to steady his legs.

He called out Shelley's name and heard nothing back.

Slowly he walked to the side where her face was and touched it. It was still warm, and he placed his own face next to hers. She was not breathing.

Unsure of what to do, his first thoughts were to call the paramedics, then he said, "no, the cops." Then he thought maybe I should call my brother. He stood there, freaking out with emotions running the full gamut. It seemed like an hour, but it was only a few minutes that passed.

Because of his past with Shelley, he decided to pick her up and move her into the living room. But as he walked towards it, he tripped, and her body fell onto the sofa where her left leg ended up on the floor, and her right leg leaned against a pillow.

Just as he walked around to move her, the phone rang, which scared him, and he jumped again. This time he ran back to her bedroom, found the filmy nightgown, and throw it over her body.

Jimmy knew the cops would never believe his story, let alone his brother, so he decided to leave the apartment before Noble came home from wherever she was.

As he left, he flicked off the light and walked out of the apartment. As he did, the neighbor was closing her door and only saw the shadow of his face.

Jimmy ran to his car and started driving towards the "after-hours" gig he had that night.

Jimmy could rationalize who might have killed her, but he knew he would be blamed and so he had to get out of town before anyone else saw him.

The Music Disc Murder
Chapter 17

After hearing his story, Dom asked Richard, "Did you try to contact her again? Are you sure you killed her? Did you contact the police?"

Richard replied, "No" to it all, which left Dom thinking about how he was going to help resolve this situation.

For the next several days, Dom told Richard to stay low, and if he went to any of his old haunts to keep it light.

Dom's neighbors knew of Richard and his car since he had lived there for many years before moving to California. So they weren't troubled or concerned when it was not there.

Richard spent his days driving to his old record store, Record Revolution on Coventry Road in Cleveland Heights.

Known for its rock stars presence, anyone might run into Patty Smith to The Who. It was the hippest hippie and free-thinking joint in town.

He hung out there for hours going through the bins minding his business, and since new owners had bought the store, they did not know him and where he worked.

To Richard, he seemed to be on vacation. He forgot all about Shelley, California, and what may have happened, and he went back to Dom's house each day and watched T.V., ate dinner and chatted with his uncle. Life was good, or at least Richard thought so.

There had been reports that Dom was involved in one way or another with the Cleveland Mayfield Gang.

This group did have connections to the Chicago Outfit, but Dom never let on what he did, if anything, for them.

Nor was there ever any convicted crimes by Dom and his neighbors never thought of him as anything but a nice guy who was married to Hanna and went to work each day and took care of his yard.

As it turned out, Dom worked for a waste and trash company that also was a cement company, by the name of Cleveland Waste and Cement, otherwise known as CWC.

The company was the largest known employer in the city, with over 1300 teamster members.

CWC was heavily involved in the city's politics, with additional influences over other cities that included Columbus, Detroit, South Bend Indiana, and Buffalo New York.

With what information Dom got from Richard, and partly because of the great distance between Cleveland and LA, the material gathered and obtained from the Los Angeles Police Department reported some information that could implicate Richard in Shelley's murder.

From this, Dom only saw a few options to help out his nephew, since he was laying low in Cleveland and couldn't take any chances of the police snooping around.

After contacting one of the Gang's "made members" for assistance to the situation, he was told to bring Richard to a warehouse on Euclid, on a particular day and time.

When that day came, Dom told Richard that everything was going to be alright and that he was taking him to see someone who could help.

After dropping off Richard, Dom never heard from his nephew again. Neither did he ever think that anything bad had come to his nephew.

However, upon asking about Richard's whereabouts from his connection, Moses Leonardo, Moses told him, "not to worry, everything was taken care of."

He then asked Dom if Richard had driven to his house, and Dom said, "yes." So after a few days had passed when Dom was at work, a truck with no name or markings on its door panels or hood drove up to the driveway with a sun-glassed hooded man.

It backed up to the car and loaded the Camaro onto the bed of the truck. There was never any more conversation about whatever happened to the Camaro or about Richard again.

Unfortunately, amongst the Families, there was always the fear of connection to any gang member or crime committed. So most crime families would try and close those gaps before any loose tongues could finger a member.

In his final investigation of Richard, the Lieutenant was able to trace his whereabouts to Cleveland, but after that, the trail ran cold. No one knew anything about this guy from California or what may have happened to him, and Long decided to discontinue his search.

The Lieutenant had contacted the Cleveland Police, who, upon their own investigation, believed that he was sent to Italy or was hiding in some other location.

No one ever thought that he might be "taken out" by the Mob.

In the investigation by the Cleveland Police, Dom did tell them that his nephew came "home" for a vacation and that as far as he knew, he returned to Los Angeles to take on the job that he had recently been promoted to.

However, no one was able to ever locate Richard in Los Angeles or any other place in California.

Furthermore, no one ever searched any more after that, and the disappearance of Richard continued to be a mystery to the police in both Cleveland and Los Angeles.

The Music Disc Murder
Chapter 18

The coroner confirmed that Shelley's death was a homicide, though it could have been accidental. However, it could have been a reckless act by another person, even if there was no intention to cause harm. In the end, the coroner did not rule out murder, so it prompted the police to investigate Shelley's death in several ways.

Hence the coroner's findings only convoluted the case for the police because of the handprints on her throat. They couldn't find a match.

Lieutenant Long and Sergeant Murphy knew how it would be ruled. After all, all the evidence from the crime scene proved that, and so there was no need for further confirmation. Yet, it was standard practice to see if they could find the murderer.

Long was befuddled by what type of girl Shelley Wright seemed to be. Was she a loose girl in Hollywood, or was it just that way in the '70s, he thought.

But as Long and Murphy uncovered, the time between her affair with Rudy and being the Hollywood butterfly, to when she started dating, Bobby was not very long.

It was the record label parties and events that occurred one after another that pushed Bobby and Shelley together like on a train heading for the station. Dreadfully, they never got the chance to be a real couple.

Even so, Long attended the funeral, held at the Church of the Good Shepherd.

Shelley's parents were deeply saddened over their only daughter's death. They like almost everyone else, could not understand.

Mr. Wright held up Mrs. Wright as the priest asked everyone to stand and bow their heads after the mass.

It was a terrible day for all those in attendance.

Shelley Noble could not stop crying, as Jeffrey held her to him. Carol and Ruth were hopeless as they stood and wept. Jordan sobbed as Steve placed his arms around her. And standing in the back was Evie, Carlo, David and some of the other Music Disc personnel. Also attending were record label guests and some local retailers, including Rudy.

Bobby, who was dressed in all black with sunglasses on, stood alone and off to the side, away from everyone else.

His heart ached beyond anything he had ever felt before. His love for Shelley was now gone way too soon, and the flicker of that flame in his life had been extinguished even before they had a chance to be a true couple.

Later that day, Rudy stopped the Sergeant to tell him that he knew who did it and that it was "Jimmy."

The Sergeant told Rudy that they were trying to locate him at that moment for questioning. Then he said to Rudy, "Thank You" and went to his squad car.

After the funeral, Mr. Wright asked Bobby if he'd come to the house, but Bobby declined but asked if he could some other time.

Mr. Wright said, "I understand, and you are more than welcome to come by anytime since we know that Shelley loved you very much, and we feel that you are our son-in-law, and thank you for everything you had done for her.

Bobby started to sob, and Mr. Wright placed his arms over Bobby's shoulders and said, "OK."

Then Bobby walked away.

At the wake in Beverly Hills, at Wright's home, more questions concerning Richard and his whereabouts in addition to Jimmy flowed from most attendees.

These two guys had vanished, and it just seemed to be out of the ordinary that two of the men in her life would not be there.

A multitude of questions and statements were reflected in conversations by the Music Disc people, as did her parents and of course, the cops. Yet, no one was sure about anything or anybody that was involved with Shelley.

Bobby waited until everyone was gone from the gravesite and knelt by the freshly placed flowers.

As he looked at the tombstone, he began weeping uncontrollably. In all his life, Bobby had never cried like this before.

Lost, he didn't know what he was going to do next.

The Music Disc Murder
Chapter 19

At the home office of MAR/Music Disc, Richard never
reported onboard as originally scheduled.

There was never a phone call to tell Human
Resources that he declined the job. There were no
messages, and when they reached out to Music Disc
in Sun Valley, neither Steve or Carol could shed any
light on his disappearance.

HR once tried to contact Richard through his last
known phone number only to hear, "The number you
have reached has been disconnected. There is no
new number listed."

At Music Disc, the mood for several weeks remained
somber. No one seemed to shake the death of
Shelley from their minds or conversation. Eventually,
Steve had another open meeting to discuss her death,
which finally put it to rest, and everyone began to get
back to normal.

The L.A. police continued to look for clues, and Bobby
called almost every other day to the consulate, only
to hear that there was nothing new to report.

Though once the consulate did find out that Jimmy
may have been jailed over an incident with a girl. But
nothing more than that.

The Mexican authorities reported to the consulate that there was a woman thought to be a hooker who was last seen with Jimmy, but nothing else.

In an after-report years later, it seems that Jimmy found himself in the arms of the Ensenada Police Captain's girlfriend at the Cantina, where she worked part-time, and they hit it off.

Unfortunately for Jimmy, Sylvia bragged about it to another girl who told her boyfriend, who then told the Ensenada Captain.

Jimmy was one of the few American's living the good life on a beach in a rented cottage when the police came and arrested him, while he was in bed with Sylvia.

And while she paid the price for sleeping with the American, she survived the ordeal with a black eye and bruised ribs.

Jimmy, on the other hand, was told to pay up $5000.00 to get out of jail, and so he called his brother. The problem was that he never told Bobby where he was.

After waiting several weeks, living in jail on water, beans, and tortillas, Jimmy was told by the Captain that he was tired of receiving no money from anyone.

Jimmy was sent off to be part of a road gang, fixing the Baja roads, which were the worse in the country.

From that point, Jimmy was never heard from again.

His whereabouts were never reported to anyone, so no one knew if he was alive or died.

In the meantime, living alone after years of roommates and his wife, there was some regret from Bobby regarding his breakup with Evie, but it probably was more to do with the loneliness that he now felt without his brother or Shelley in his life.

Though Bobby continuously questioned if his brother could have killed Shelley, knowing how much he loved her, his answer was always the same, "perhaps."

The Music Disc Murder
Chapter 20

The forgotten death of Charlotte did not go unnoticed by the South Bay police or family.

Not one office friend or associate could understand her murder. She was not a party girl or someone who ran around with anyone. She did her job, was always on time and dressed fashionably without being a tramp or shameful.

Charlotte worked at the company that made airline parts and electronics. She planned to meet her friend Barbara Lutz at the jazz club that night. They were to meet up for a late dinner around 8. So, after work, Charlotte went home, took a nap, and got ready shortly after 7.

By 9 o'clock, Charlotte knew that Barb was not coming and ordered her meal of fish and chips, right before the band was scheduled to go on around 10 PM.

Preceding this, Charlotte made eye contact with a guy who had long blonde hair sitting at the bar. It was an innocent connection, like a hello, and nothing more. But the guy came over as he was heading to the stage and said, "Hi, my name is Jimmy, what's yours?"

Surprised, Charlotte smiled and told him her name, and that was that.

After the set, Charlotte wondered if she should go home since she was alone and didn't like being there by herself.

Sensing her discomfort, Jimmy said to her as he walked past her table, "I'll be right back if you don't mind?"

To which she said, "Okay" and smiled as she watched him pass by her table.

The evening seemed to go by quickly for Charlotte even though it was well past her normal bedtime. She was absorbed by Jimmy and his stories of the rock and roll business.

As he blurted out story after story, he asked her if she would like to go to Mexico for a few days, since he was going there to perform with a band in Ensenada.

Charlotte had never been down to Baja and was thrilled that someone was willing to take her there.

When the club closed for the night and Jimmy followed Charlotte back to her apartment, there was no intention of taking Charlotte to Baja.

Jimmy was stringing Charlotte along to bed her down for the night. He needed some company after the situation at Shelley's.

Charlotte was feeling giddy after a few drinks and longed for some attention that Jimmy was all too willing to fulfill.

Soon enough, though, she found out what Jimmy was really after, and it wasn't just a kiss or hug.

Though not unfamiliar with having sex with a stranger, Charlotte was not anxious to bed Jimmy.

Though the attention she was receiving felt good, she seemed to not be up to par with Jimmy and during the sexual encounter, sweetness turned to abuse, as Jimmy unleashed his violent side.

Miscalculations occurred that by the time Jimmy left, Charlotte was not breathing.

It seemed that holding someone by the throat during sex is not a great way of showing emotion unless you intend to do bodily harm.

When the cops found Charlotte's body, handprints were still visible from someone who took out his rage on the poor girl.

Jimmy's wrath was beyond contrition.

What was that jealousy and possessiveness that overcame people to the point of a criminal act of violence?

Except for Sylvia, Jimmy's acts of love were nothing more than anger. In Sylvia, he found his match when she tied him up and beat him with a cactus leather belt and buckle. So, when he was thrown in jail, it was a blessing in disguise, or he thought it was at that time.

The Music Disc Murder
Chapter 21

As the spinning record business of the '70s spun out of control, Evie was on the fast track of her own with Sir Taylor that, in a way, took the record business by surprise, especially after the merger.

After the divorce was final, Evie moved to New York to be closer to Sir Douglas, since he moved much of his operation to the "Big Apple." Taylor maintained transatlantic businesses to ensure that his "record company" succeeded, and even though he trusted Evie to run the film side, his main focus was where and what Carlo was doing.

Following the divorce and after the passing of Shelley, Bobby began to drink more and earlier in the day and was discreet in his frequent misuse.

Evie and Bobby sold their home, and Bobby moved into a guest house in Sherman Oaks.

Small, but adequate, the owners kept watch and maintained his house when he was traveling.

Set back behind the main house, there was a walkway from the street directly to his front door.

Included in the property was a huge pool that on many a day, Bobby found himself plonked down in a chair nursing a hangover. Sometimes there was a lady friend who shared his bed and pool, but mostly it was himself.

The industry with its loose women and easy money became Bobby's new best friends, and while Carlo kept tabs on him, it was only when David stepped in that turned Bobby around.

Feeling sorry for himself since Shelley's demise, Bobby couldn't get a grasp on life. He was partying in Vegas much of the time and losing thousands of dollars monthly to either the gaming tables or to the women that he shacked up with.

David, who frequently gambled in Vegas found Bobby one night, slumped over a card table at the Frontier on an extended weekend.

David and his wife were able to get Bobby back to his room to sleep off his drunken state, and when he awoke the next day, it was time for an intervention, according to David.

Bobby couldn't let it go of what had happened. He was in "lost territory" as David put it, with his brother's disappearance and the murder of Shelley, along with never finding her killer.

Bobby sometimes thought he would go mad.

It was primarily with David's help; however, that Bobby slowly made his way back to sanity, changing his lifestyle and moving forward.

The Music Disc Murder
Chapter 22

Nathan Brown, THE "BELAFONTE" up and comer, was like Noble, fair-skinned because of mixed parents. Fortunately for his dark green eyes, it set him apart from both white and black actors, and because of his complexion, he ended up doing bit parts for almost all nationalities.

A young man on a mission in the entertainment business, he started out working at Universal Studios, tending to actors, executives, and fans alike.

Pleasant enough on the outside, Nathan had a ruthless streak inside that only a few knew about: one of them was Noble.

On too many occasions did he show his true color of being belligerent and brutal in his response to something that he didn't like.

Noble, in fact, told him one day after he was about to hit her that "it would be the last thing he ever did and that she would cut off his privates to make a point."

After that, Nathan never again raised so much as a finger or voice her way.

Two days before Shelley Wright's murder, he was performing live on stage in a Cinderella Play at the Dorothy Chandler Pavilion, where both Shelley's attended in support of Nathan.

After the late-night drinks and dinner following the show, Noble had arranged to meet up with Carlo. So, she dashed off to some hotel in Beverly Hills to do just that.

This left Nathan and Shelley sharing a cab back to her place.

Nathan had intended to drop Shelley off and then head off to his apartment; however, on the way, Nathan convinced Shelley to allow himself to come in for a nightcap.

Shelley had said in the past that she didn't want to have a relationship with Nathan, particularly with her ongoing affair with Bobby. However, she suddenly found herself in a pickle.

More times than not, when Bobby was out of town, and unfortunately, when Shelley was alone, she might get caught up in the moment. This time it was Nathan.

A sweet talker whose never-ending repertoire was played on his other girlfriends, he convinced Shelley to allow him to spend the night stating that he was too damn drunk to take a cab back to his home.

Shelley, who didn't want to upset him or Noble, said, "yes."

In Nathan's mind, this afforded another opportunity to sleep with Shelley. Sensing his intentions, she told him that under no circumstance would she allow this to happen.

During that night, he tried several times to make love to her, but to no avow, she did not permit this.

To say that Nathan was upset was an understatement. He was not used to any female rejecting his intentions.

Cussing and carrying on out in the hallway, Shelley could only sleep for a little while as she was afraid that he would somehow unlock her bedroom door and try to have sex with her.

In the morning, Nathan was gone but had left a note cursing her again and calling her a bitch and a teaser and that she would get hers.

Shelley was afraid to tell anyone, mainly Noble or even Bobby, for fear of any recourse from either of them. Not that Noble would cause much of a fuss, but Bobby might go off the deep end on her or Nathan.

When Sergeant Murphy found this threatening note in Shelley's journal, he didn't think much about it.

Murphy assumed it had to be either Richard or Jimmy. But after verifying that it was neither of their handwriting, he began to dig deeper and found out that it was another friend or boyfriend that left this.

It seemed that everywhere that Shelley went, there was a trail of men who wanted her or who might want to take out some sort of revenge on her.

Nathan was enamored with Shelley from the moment he saw her. Despite his long list of girlfriends, he lusted after her, but tried to keep it in check as to not upset the relationship with Noble.

The casual meetings at the Workshop were innocent enough as they all laughed and joked after the sessions. But even when Nathan was making love to Noble, he could see Shelley, and so it became an obsession when he was around her.

Noble sensed something was happening and asked him outright, which he denied. But that didn't stop Noble from telling Shelley to be careful when she was alone with him.

Unlike the episode with Jimmy screwing her after they broke up and she was drunk, Nathan always seemed to be the gentleman, and so Shelley never took it seriously that he wanted her.

Yet Sergeant Murphy obtained a search warrant for Nathan's apartment, and he and a few officers went to his place and found Nathan home.

When he opened the door at 10:30 AM, the sleepily Nathan answered his door in only a pair of boxer shorts, rubbing his eyes. It appeared that the Sergeant had woken him up from a late evening.

Surprised after the Sergeant's introduction, he immediately woke himself up to what was happening as the officers barged in.

The young white girl, who was no older than 19, as the police found out, was sleeping with Nathan. She walked out from the bedroom, stark naked unashamed of her composure, and said, "Nathan, what are these guys doing?"

Nathan turned and said, "Get your clothes on. We are done here."

With that, the girl went back into the bedroom, got dressed, and left, but not before one of the officers obtained her name, phone number, and address.

Searching Nathan's apartment, Murphy found several hand-written notes addressed to Shelley that were never given to her.

A few naked photos of Shelley that were taken by a Polaroid and a sweater that, according to Nathan, he couldn't remember who it belonged to or how he had gotten it.

Murphy instructed his officers to seize all the items in question for examination and substantiation. Then he told Nathan to get dressed as he was being escorted to the station for further questioning.

The Music Disc Murder
Chapter 23

Nathan and Noble were quite the pair, studying parts together, going to star-studded events, and getting acting parts in several of the same movies.

However, after their initial relationship cooled to the point of just sex on occasion, Nathan lusted after Shelley and told her so.

Shelley, fearful of telling Noble, said nothing but threatened Nathan that she would. Several times after coming over to spend the night with Noble, he would privately tell Shelley that he wanted her.

After the third time, Shelley made it a point to lock her bedroom door and never again be alone with Nathan.

Somehow, Nathan had taken her sweater accidentally at either a concert or movie. However, she never knew it and Nathan had forgotten about it and hung it in his closet.

With Murphy questioning Nathan at the station, he began to sense that Nathan could have been the culprit in the murder, but it would be a long shot in comparison with Richard and Jimmy. Nevertheless, he didn't want to rule it out either.

Nathan, as Murphy determined, was no murderer but was definitely a womanizer, an actor looking to be famous and would do anything in his power to achieve just that.

Therefore, he let him go but told Nathan to let his office know if he was taking any roles outside of the Los Angeles area.

When the investigation was completed, Lieutenant Long received the report from Murphy about Nathan and filed it away.

Long told the Sergeant about the death of Charlotte that it seemed to resemble the death of Shelley with the same "M O."

Long had been scouting the other police departments, and her murder popped up in the daily report that the Los Angeles and Orange County sheriffs' offices all shared.

If it hadn't been for a copy being placed in his own basket, he might not have ever seen the report.

In reality, these types of report would normally go to the on-duty Detectives to investigate, so it was just by chance that Long saw it and thought there might be a connection.

The Lieutenant did speak with Bobby after his return from Mexico and the discussions with the consulate.

Bobby did not hold anything back from telling Long what had taken place in his search, and what he knew, but the police never found out any more than what the consulate reported.

As Murphy and Long read the reports and compared them, they concluded that Jimmy might have been the killer since he had disappeared and seemed to be the man with Charlotte the evening she was murdered.

Though any of the men involved could have been the perpetrator, the police did not rule out the possibility of someone other than these three that could have been the murderer.

The Music Disc Murder
Chapter Epilogue

The murders of Shelley Wright and Charlotte Fleming were never fully resolved since neither Richard nor Jimmy were ever found alive again.

Based on the evidence found and the neighbor's report, there was a theory that Jimmy had watched Richard come out of Shelley's apartment after the two had returned from the alcoholic and pot-smoking concert they had attended together. Technically just a record label event and not a date, Jimmy would never have known this and then killed her.

Somehow Richard had convinced Shelley to make love during their time of being high together, but this was after he had gotten a little rough with her during their time in the bedroom.

Though it wouldn't have been considered rape, it was a damn close thing to it, since Shelley was alarmed by Richards's forcefulness and determination, going through the motions to just let him have his way with her.

On the other hand, Richard felt like he finally achieved his goal and that Shelley would love him forever, even though it was the furthest from her mind.

Nevertheless, Jimmy waited till Richard had gone before using the spare key that he had made and walked in through the halls to Shelley's room, where he found her naked and spent.

Jimmy may have thought that she was dead and that the cops and his brother would never believe him and would, therefore, blame him for her murder.

His dilemma got the best of him and decided to leave town before anyone knew that he had been there. But in his haste, he felt obligated to move her from the bed to the couch to maybe deflect any wrongdoing. And then he threw the robe over her as he bolted for the door.

Charlotte Fleming's murder was also never solved, as the long-haired musician was never seen again, and the police had no other evidence to go on.

Her murder was a result of a broken neck, much like Shelley's. Some say that it was two different guys who killed them and not the same one, but it propelled wild speculation as the years went by.

Jimmy Columbo was never found alive after notification was given to the American Consulate that he was in the Ensenada jail. Nor was there any other bribe or ransom request ever sent to Bobby.

Richard Graydon's whereabouts remain a mystery.

He never reported to the position at MAR/Music Disc that he was promoted to, and no one in his hometown of Lincoln Park, has seen him after his car went missing from his Uncle's driveway that night.

Bobby never got over Shelley's death and stayed single and mostly depressed when alone. Although he continued to work as a salesman in the industry, he went from company to company almost every two years due to mergers or companies going out of business.

His true happiness since he gave up drinking and gambling was helping kids at the local Big Brothers center.

Evie and Taylor did get married, and she quit the business to become the mother of his children along with their own. And ElectroDisc still owns Music Disc Distribution and has become a huge success in the record industry.

The future proved to be very different for Nathan as he was ousted from the movie and entertainment business due to his persistence of being a lover of women.

After his last film he was starring in, he bedded down the leading actress who he had given drugs to and she overdosed. This led to his downfall.

Noble, on the other hand, found herself starring in a TV soap opera for the rest of her life, which paid her handsomely. She never married but settled for only two men in her life – her lover Carlo and her best friend, Bobby.

About the Author

Michael lives in the Tampa Bay area with his wife, Laura. They have a daughter and one granddaughter at the time of this writing. His resume is varied, initially with 30 years in the music industry, holding many positions: President, Vice President of International Sales, Vice President, and General Manager with various Major and Independent Record Companies during the 70s, 80s, and 90s. He is the current owner of ITI Music Corporation (ITI Records and Warrant Music) and credited with over 100 titles released. He also retired as a Navy Supply Officer after serving 35 years. Taught Social Science in Middle and High schools in Pasco County. World traveler, he has visited most of Europe and Asia, including Tahiti, Australia, and New Zealand. Most favorite spots in the world: Hawaii, Japan, England, France, and Italy.

Read more at www.itimusic.live.

www.ingramcontent.com/pod-product-compliance
Lightning Source LLC
Chambersburg PA
CBHW030519260626
47157CB00005B/1813